HER COMEBACK

LOLA WEST

Not every one has an Iwa...

They are not as lucky as me.

NOTE TO READER

The first half of this book, If you Love Someone was originally the prequel to the Big Sky Cowboys Series, but it is also the first half of Kat and Billy's love story - and well, the first and the second half belonged together in one place. Their love story is best when read all together.

So if you read Tofu Cowboy you're about to go back in time for a bit...

Xo,

Lola

IF YOU LOVE SOMEONE

PART 1

1

BILLY

She would always be mine.

That's what I told myself as I looked at Kat curled up next to me in the cab of my truck. We were driving a little over two hours to Bozeman, MT for the biggest performance she'd booked yet. She looked so serene next to me, her curvy little body curled to fit on the seat, her bare feet and red painted toes resting in my lap. I couldn't help myself from caressing her calves. Just the feel of her skin under my fingertips quickened my pulse. I was tempted to run my hand up her leg and take a peek under her skirt. But I knew I wouldn't stop there and she really needed her rest. Tonight was a big night for her. So, as much as I hungered to slip my fingers under her panties, I wanted to care for her more.

My mother was convinced Kat and I were fated. She used to say that Kat was my girl, the one made just for me. Before she died, my mother told the story of the first time I touched Kat to anyone who would listen.

"Inseparable from the start," she'd say.

The way my mother told it, Kat was six months old and I was just over a year. Our families were neighbors for a generation, so Kat's mom, Miriam and my mom, Molly, had always been friendly. When they had babies within months of each other, they grew even closer. In the early months of our lives, our mothers often had coffee together, but they didn't put us in the same playpen until Kat could sit up on her own. Apparently, the first day they threw us together, I grabbed a hold of Kat's hand and wouldn't let go. I was barely verbal at the time, but when my mother picked me up to leave, I began to cry and scream, "No, mine," over and over again. Our whole lives, there was an oral history of our destiny. My mother called it the kind of love that was written in the stars.

Maybe for other people that would have felt stifling, the pressure to love the girl (or the boy) next door. But in our case, it was undeniable. If you asked me, there were no other girls. Of course, in the beginning we were just friends. When we were kids Kat was a tomboy. She'd pull her heavy mane of red hair back in a ponytail, and she and I would muck about catching frogs and climbing trees all over my parents' ranch. Sometimes, we'd let Luke, the eldest of my brothers hangout with us. My other three siblings weren't born yet or they were too young. So, mostly it was just her and me, stirring up trouble. Even then, the only thing Kat did without me was play the guitar.

Eventually, we weren't little kids anymore. I got taller and my voice cracked. Kat started wearing skirts and lip gloss. When we were thirteen, I was standing with a group of guys and a kid named Walt said that he wanted to ask Kat to the middle school dance. I didn't even think. I just punched him square in the nose. I might have even growled, "Mine." I took Kat to the middle school dance, still just as friends. But I held her hand, danced with her for the first time, and told her she looked pretty.

When she was a sophomore and I was a junior in high school, I finally kissed her. At that point I'd been lusting after her for years. Neither one of us dated anyone else, ever. It wasn't that there weren't any interested parties, both Kat and I had offers, but even before we kissed, we were together. We drove to school together. We ate lunch together. Our families even had dinner together. Kat always sat next to me. It was just a given. In those days I looked for excuses to touch her. I'd hug her good morning for a few extra seconds. I'd take her to a movie and sit with my legs real wide, so our knees tapped. I'd offer my hand when she was climbing out of my truck, anything to be close. Then, one night when I went to pick her up from her job as a waitress at the Conway Cafe, I couldn't bear to just be her best friend any longer. I had to have more. That first taste of her lips was addicting.

After that, we spent hours in the loft of my father's barn, kissing and talking about life. Kat had big dreams. She wanted to be a singer, to write songs that affected people. I didn't have those kinds of thoughts. I loved the land. I was happy with the life I was born into. Early morning on horseback, herding cattle was good enough for me, but dawn between Kat's thighs was better. So, before my momma died, I just thought that if Kat's dreams came true, I would tag along.

That solution was harder now. So much had happened since those early days of kisses and petting that lead to licks, sucking and eventually the feeling of sliding my cock deep inside her warm wet pussy. My mother died and my family needed me. I wasn't free anymore. I couldn't just pick up and leave. Maybe, if it was just Luke and Wyatt. They were both in high school. They could fend for themselves. But I had Cody and Sarah to think about, and they were only ten. And my father, he was a mess still from losing my momma. How could he run the ranch by himself? I was trapped in Montana. So, if Kat's dreams came true tomorrow, mine would have to die. But honestly, what was the likelihood of that. How many small-town girls get famous overnight?

And even if she did, she would always be mine, right? I was strong enough to let her go, wasn't I? Or maybe she'd choose me, just like I'd choose her. If I had a choice.

Her feet twitched in my lap. And then she rubbed them together and they grazed over my dick. A long time slave to her touch, it woke coming to half mast, always needy for her attention. With her eyes still closed she smiled and bit her lip. Then, she moved her foot with much more intentional targeting of my hardening situation, running the pad of her foot back and forth over it.

"Hmm..." She teased, "Is that a hard on in your pocket, or are you smuggling a really unripe, strangely large banana in your pants?"

She was a saucy little thing. I poked back, "You wake that beast, you better be ready to make good. You may have been napping for the last few hours, but I've been daydreaming about that sweet treat you keep under your skirt."

She giggled and then pulled her feet back, curling them under her bottom and sitting up.

"How much further?" She asked.

"Thirty minutes, tops."

She'd slept most of the drive. Kat was one of those people who napped easily. I was not. It worked for her. A little nap refreshed her whole attitude, and the gig in Bozeman had her so jazzed that she hadn't slept much. Nervous energy continued to buzz under her skin. Her excitement was like a living thing causing her to physically vibrate in place. I worked hard to try to be in the moment for her, but my still hard cock enjoyed watching her breasts bounce, and when my little head got a hold of my brain, he was hard to ignore.

Fuck.

I took a deep cleansing breath and tried to refocus my energy. I spoke to my inner caveman. *Get it together. You're driving.*

He wasn't buying it.

Must have pussy.

I could almost feel her tight and wet around me.

Yes, I hear you, very sexy girl but it's not a good time. Focus, driving.

I glanced at Kat, wondering if she realized how much I wanted her right then. She was looking out the window clearly oblivious to my sex drive, her mind cluttered with thoughts of her gig.

My caveman humphed, *Fine, love girl.*

With my shit under control, I turned to Kat.

"What are you thinking about?" I asked, knowing full well that I was in for an earful of Kat's musings about the potential for exposure she might get by playing this gig. Sometimes, when you love someone, you listen, even when you've heard it all before.

*****

A FEW HOURS LATER, I watched her climb the stage. She looked the part, sweet but sexy in a jean skirt, cowboy boots, and a pale yellow top that complemented her shiny and smooth red hair. The venue, Harry's Feeding Station, didn't seem like the kind of place a person got their start in. It was an old gas station that had been turned into a honky-tonk eatery/bar. The walls were covered in music memorabilia and license plates. There was also a lot of black paint and metal. It was like what you would get if a TGI Fridays ate a nightclub. The ambiance was not for my taste, but apparently, Harry—or whatever the owner's real name was—had an ear for talent and if you wanted to hear good music in Bozeman, it was the joint. Someone named Laurie, who worked for Maybe-Harry, had seen Kat at a county festival a couple of months ago and asked her if she wanted to do an opening set before a larger band.

Laurie made it clear that the pay wouldn't be much, but Kat was over the moon about getting paid to sing at all. She didn't even have a demo yet. I'd been saving my pennies to give her the money for her demo on her birthday. I had to admit, it was exciting. The band Kat was opening for was local to Bozeman, so a crowd of local fans was being exposed to her, which meant they might be interested in seeing her another time. Also, I was the tiniest bit comforted by the local feel of it all. It mitigated my fears that Kat would catapult directly from this show on to something bigger and better. I wanted that for her, I did... just not right now. The crowd was rowdy like they might heckle if Kat didn't please them. It was nothing like her loyal fan base at Sadie's, our hometown joint.

While I was riled up and anxious for her, Kat seemed cool as a cucumber. She wrapped her slender fingers around the base of the microphone and said, "Before I get started, I just want to thank y'all. I'm Kat Bennett. I know I'm young and unfamiliar and I..." She took a deep, contemplative breath, "Well, I just really appreciate you giving me a chance to play my music for you." She offered the room a smile.

Kat had many smiles. I knew them all, but I knew this one really well. This smile was usually reserved for me. It was a little sexy smile—a smile that seduced. She was wooing them. Like always, she followed up this particular smile by nibbling on her lower lip for a second. A part of me started to feel uncomfortable that she was sexing it up on stage, even if it was subtle. What man wants to watch other men ogle his woman? But then, right before she started singing, she looked for me. We agreed that I would stand by the bar where there was a little light so that if she needed me for any reason, she would know where to find me. I didn't know if she could really see me, but she was looking right at me. She strummed her guitar and started to sing.

I couldn't look away. I'd seen Kat sing so many times before, but this was different. She was bare and raw. Her sound was soft but resonate. Her eyes were closed, her focus inward as if she were calling on her soul to make her music for her. The room fell quiet as the crowd started to listen. She was undeniable.

If anyone with clout was watching, my girl wasn't going to just be mine anymore.

KAT

The audience at Harry's Feeding Station wasn't what I was used to. I mean, in all honesty, I really only knew three kinds of audiences and none of them were particularly professional:

1. The audience in my high school gymnasium.
2. The audience at Sadie's, which was basically the same audience from the gym, only with beers.
3. Audiences at the county fair, which consisted of people eating lunch or resting their feet.

But even if this group was unfamiliar, I had to charm them, and not just because I'd graduated from high school, so my number one audience was no longer accessible to me. I had to charm the people at Harry's Feeding Station because I needed to make a living as a musician. I couldn't imagine a life where I did anything other than sing. Music was like breathing for me. If I didn't play every day, my soul started to hyperventilate. I know some people have big dreams because they want out of where they came from, but that wasn't my story. I loved where I came from. I didn't need to be famous (I wasn't even sure I'd like being famous), I just wanted to create music, to let it pour out of me... the happy, the beautiful, the sad. Music was oxygen.

The only thing better than music was Billy. Big, strong, blue-eyed Billy was my heartbeat. He was the blood in my veins. He was the engine that kept everything moving, the energy that brought me joy, laughter, and pleasure. Billy was where the music began. He was in every note. The way women inspired male artists throughout history, Billy was my muse. But he was more than that, he was my center, my home. For as long as I could remember, Billy was part of me in a way that defies understanding. I just knew that, without him, I was less.

Which was why, standing on the stage at Harry's Feeding Station, looking out over the rowdy and unfamiliar crowd, I called on him. I looked to the spot where we had agreed he would be standing, confirming his actual presence. Past the sea of darkness at my feet, I could see him. It was hard to make out the details, but my cowboy was standing just where he said he'd be, facing me, leaning against the bar, burly arms crossed over his chest, emanating a protective-ness like a bouncer outside a raging club.

Once I confirmed his actual presence, I looked for him inside myself. I'd never called on my love for Billy before, but I often tried to call on my emotions while I sang. Music needs passion and feeling to be good. Just like actors express the complexities of the human experience, good musicians make you feel. And on that stage, I felt Billy all over me, so that's what I gave the audience. I let go of my need to impress the people in front of me and willed my memories of Billy on my skin to coax the music from me—his lips on my lips, the way he cradled my face when we kissed, the pressure of his fingers as he kneaded my shoulders, gripped my ass, tickled the place where my shirt met my jeans, the silk of his dark chocolate hair threading through my hands and the slick of his tongue when his face was between my thighs. Every song rose up and crested like a climax, thick with need and passion. When my music was like this, I was just a conduit. What the people were hearing wasn't the songs or cords I'd written; it was my love for Billy, the boy who owned my heart.

When I finished the set, there was that perfect pause. The moment when the sound waves from your last note peter out, and for one extraordinary beat, the room is wondrously silent. You only get that silence when you're so good that you've completely captured the audience's attention. They're not talking to their friends or drinking their beers. They're just watching you, feeling your music in their souls. What followed that silence was a crashing applause. I stood there, holding my guitar, grinning so hard my face hurt. I felt the sweat on my lower back. My blood raced and my breaths were hurried. Performing was always a rush. Performing with Billy on my mind was an explosion. When the cheer of the crowd quieted to a rumble, I pulled the microphone to my mouth, "Thank you, you were all awesome. Hope to see you again. And in case you forgot," I paused to wink and smile. "I'm Kat Bennett."

The stage was just a platform at the front of the room, so there was no escaping the crowd. Somewhere, a lighting tech turned the stage lights down and the house lights up. I made my way into a little swarm of people wanting to chat with me, mostly new-found fans. It felt exciting to be inspirational enough that people wanted to shake my hand or find out more.

I peeked over the shoulder of a woman with long shiny brown hair who was asking me where she could buy my music, to see Billy making his way through the crowd towards me. I turned back to her, "I'm still working on getting established," I said. "But I have a couple of videos on YouTube. If you want to give me your email or your card or whatever, I could contact you when there is something more."

She liked that idea, so I waited while she reached into her purse, taking another peek at Billy who was just a few strides from me now. I saw Billy's face contort with rage before I felt the random man's hands on me. He was behind me, pulling on my hips. I tried to step away, towards the woman with the long shiny hair, but the man pressed me against his hips and his torso. My skin crawled. I smelled the bar on him and I felt his hot sticky breath on the shell of my ear when he said, "You're awfully sexy for such a little thing."

Almost immediately, I was yanked away from the man. Billy locked eyes with me. His baby blues, normally so solid and calm, were dark and stormy. After a split-second inspection to make sure I was alright, he spun back on the man whose hands had been on me. He didn't yell or threaten. Actually, he didn't say anything. His demeanor was unlike anything I'd ever seen from him. My Billy was cool as a cucumber, an unflappable, solid kind of man. The Billy stalking my violator was a barbarian—a beast threatening with growls, not words.

With the hulk of Billy descending on him, the man nervously threw his hands up and said, "I didn't know she was your girl, buddy. Okay?"

Billy cold-cocked him with one vicious punch and then, with the man sprawled at his feet, Billy snarled his answer, "So not okay."

3

BILLY

The door of Harry's Feeding Station slapped closed behind me. We trekked through the dark parking lot without even acknowledging each other. Ten paces in front of me, Kat was in a huff. She could be as pissed as she wanted to be. I get it. It was her big night and the last thing she needed was her adrenaline-fueled boyfriend causing a scene and getting thrown out of the venue. But to be clear, I didn't start that fight. I ended it. Yes, she was my girl and someone else touching her filled me with so much rage that I acted without caution, but that dude was an ass, one hundred percent. If I saw him touch another woman the way he touched Kat, it would have upset me. You couldn't just rub yourself on a girl that wasn't yours. That was unacceptable shit.

Kat got to the truck and stood at the door, waiting for me to unlock it. There was a soft glow from the floodlights on the side of the building that lit Kat up as she stood there. Her nostrils were flared, her lips were tightly pursed, her arms were crossed, and her hip was flared out. Everything about her body language screamed that she was fuming mad. Too bad. She could stay that way. I wasn't apologizing for what I did. No way! Carrying her guitar in one hand, I used the other to reach into my pocket and hit the unlock button on my keys. Usually, I opened the door for her and even put her in the truck, but she didn't look like she would welcome my touch. She rolled her eyes at me, pulled the handle of the truck door, climbed in, and slammed it behind her.

I had a storage box in my truck bed for her guitar, which kept it safe from the rain and meant that she always wanted me to drive her to and from her gigs. I installed it as soon as I got my truck. She cried when I showed it to her. Taking care of Kat and the things she loved was my job. I planned on it being my life's work. Just because she was angry, didn't mean her prized possession didn't matter. Gently, quieting the adrenaline in my veins, I opened the storage box and placed the guitar case inside, then padlocked it to keep it safe. I caught Kat's eye in the rear-view mirror watching me. She was mad, but she also loved me.

I got in the truck, put the key in the ignition, and started the engine. Kat was pushed as close to the passenger side door as she could be. She'd also turned to face the window. I'd seen her act like this before. Everything Kat did was full tilt. When she laughed, she roared. When she cried, she sobbed. When she loved you, she'd die for you. And when she was mad, well, she was mighty mad. So, I assumed that she was gonna be mad for a while.

We had a long drive home and I was hungry. We planned to eat at Harry's Feeding Station while listening to some music, but since that was out, I decided to stop somewhere on the way out of Bozeman. We drove in silence until I saw a place that tickled my fancy. I pulled into the parking lot and parked in the back corner. I was one of those who always parked far from other people. Strangers were dangerous. You never knew what the guy parked next to you was thinking. Also, my truck was loved and well cared for, no need for some fool to throw open his door and nick her pretty blue finish.

With the car in park and the engine off, I grumbled, "You coming?" I wanted her to come in. I didn't like leaving her in the car by herself in the dark.

Haughtily, she snapped, "I'll wait right here. Thank you very much."

So irritating, amiright? "Suit yourself, sweetheart," I quipped and jumped out of the car, slamming the door shut.

My mind raced, still high from the adrenaline of punching that jerk and annoyed that she was giving me such a hard time. I strode across the parking lot towards the door and I got about halfway before I lost my cool and turned back. She hadn't eaten all day as she had too much nervous excitement to eat earlier. She didn't have to talk to me but she was gonna fucking eat something. Back at the truck, I threw open the passenger side door and unbuckled her seat belt.

"What do you think you're doing?" she snapped.

I didn't answer. I just picked her up and tossed her over my shoulder like a bag of feed. Once she was situated, I double-checked to make sure her panties weren't showing.

"Billy," she hollered, kicking and beating her little fists against my back. "Put me down this instant."

Nope. I marched up to the door, kept her pinned to my shoulder with one hand and opened it with the other. She kept beating on me and I laughed. She was going to be so mad, but I was smiling from ear to ear. I fucking loved her. I loved her fire and her will. She was amazing. The dude behind the cash register was strangely unaffected by the appearance of a man hauling a wildcat woman through the restaurant, so I didn't feel the need to explain myself.

"I'll have two burgers, please." I heard the joy in my voice and so did Kat.

"One of those better be for me," she growled.

"Make that three, all with cheese. A large order of fries, two cokes..."

Kat pushed up on my shoulder and tried to turn so she could look at the menu, "I want an ice tea, not a coke. Also, a cookie. Get a cookie." Her order complete, she collapsed back down and returned to kicking and smacking me.

"You heard the woman. An ice tea and a cookie."

Once, I settled with the cashier, I carried Kat over to a booth and placed her down gently. She crossed her arms over her chest and continued to pout.

Still standing, but with both palms on the table, I leaned into her, "Not ready to forgive me yet, I see." I was practically singing, so amused by my own barbaric behavior.

She rolled her eyes at me.

"Suit yourself." I grabbed our cups and went to the beverage station to fill them.

4

KAT

We ate quietly in the glow of the fluorescent lights. The place was mostly empty. There was one other group of customers at the opposite end of the restaurant. It wasn't gross or anything but I took comfort in the fact that the booth we were sitting in was made of hard blue and yellow plastic from head to toe, so decades of food could be wiped away rather than collect in fabric crevices. The only sounds were the crinkles of the paper wrappings on our burgers and Billy humming my songs to himself. I knew he was trying to irritate me but also to get me to think about my performance, not what happened afterward.

At this point, I was trying really hard to stay mad at him. I couldn't believe how he took that man down with one punch. I mean, just boom and the guy was splat. They had a pretty strict policy about violence at Harry's, so as soon as Billy threw that punch, we were out. The bouncer made it clear that we would be welcomed back in the future. He also told me I was "pretty darn talented" but I couldn't be certain that they'd let me sing there again. Also, I missed out on any networking opportunities that might have presented themselves. It was a real shit show.

That said, I had to admit, the guy was an ass. I knew I was sheltered, growing up in Conway. But, my God, who walks up to a stranger and touches her like that? Gross. I mean, that dude was not okay. And Billy stopped him, like it was his job. Listen, I was beyond pissed at what Billy did and that was all I was ever going to show him, but there was this part of me, a stupid backwards silly girl part, that hadn't stopped squeezing my thighs together since he punched that guy. It was something about the shift in him. The fact that protecting me had brought out this beast, this raw animalistic man meat that I just wanted to climb and ride. And then when he threw me over his shoulder, which was infuriating, but also hot, it took every ounce of will in my being to stay mad at him when I actually wanted to straddle his lap and buck against him until I saw stars.

He finished eating first and watched me chew the last few bites of my burger before I unwrapped my cookie.

"You gonna share that with me?" he asked.

"Nope." I popped my lips around the 'p' sound.

"Come on, Kit-Kat. Just one little taste." He stuck his lower lip out, exaggerating the pout. "P-p-p-please?"

I narrowed my eyes at him. "Let me get this straight. You ruined my night and now you want my cookie too?"

One corner of his mouth lifted in mischief, and then in a low tone akin to Barry White, he said, "I always want your cookie, baby."

22

Under the table, I squeezed my thighs again. To his face, I rolled my eyes but laughed too. "You're ridiculous."

"You're delicious," he teased.

Unable to control my smile but still annoyed, I said, "I'm really mad at you." I broke off a piece of the cookie and handed it to him

He popped it in his mouth and chewed. I could see the gears in his mind churning. He didn't want me to be mad at him anymore but he wasn't sure how to get there. Huffing out a sigh, he said, "I'm sorry. I really am. I know it was a big night for you. And you wanted to hobnob and what not..."

I giggled because he said hobnob.

He continued, "But you have to give me something here. That guy was—"

I interrupted him, "An ass, but you didn't have to hit him. You could have just gotten me away."

Billy's eyes flashed stormy again. "He touched you."

"I get that, Bill." I never called him Bill unless I was pissed. "But I can handle myself."

Exasperated, he growled, "Of course you can. You didn't hit him." He was admitting he lost control. It was enough, but I'd revved up the beast, so he kept going. "What do you want me to say, Kat? That I fucking lost it? That no one touches my girl but me? That he's lucky I didn't kill him?"

Listening to him bark at me, saying that I was his, had my pulse pounding and my core clenched. I mean, what is it about being claimed that gets us all hot and bothered? It's freaking bizarre. I didn't say anything in response because I felt like if I opened my mouth, the only thing that would come out were the words, *I want you,* or maybe, *take me now, you sexy beast.*

Billy quirked his head at me. He was studying me. His eyes narrowed and then he smiled. I bit my lip. He stood, grabbed me by the hand, and for the second time that night, yanked me. And then, I was up and out of the booth and we were moving towards the door.

"The trays," I clamored, looking back at the table behind me.

"Leave it," Billy grunted

As we passed the cashier, I called out, "Sorry about the mess." Disenchanted, he shook his head as if to say, those two are cra-zy.

It was spring, but as we barreled out the door, the night air that hit my legs was cool. Billy didn't stop moving until we were at the truck, and even then, I could still feel his dark energy rising. He pressed me against the passenger door, holding my forearms to the blue metal. I squirmed to break free, but not really. He eyed me again. My breath was coming fast, heaving my breasts.

When he spoke, his voice was low and commanding. "All you have to do is say stop and I will." He released his left hand and dropped it to the bare skin on my outer thigh. His gaze followed. In the blue darkness of the back corner of the parking lot, we both watched as his fingertips started to climb. "What am I going to find up here, Kit-Kat?" he rumbled.

I whimpered, dropping my head back and closing my eyes.

"Because, I could be wrong, but I think these panties are soaked."

I shuddered. He was almost at the apex of where my leg met my pussy.

"Am I right, baby? Is your mind mad but your pussy's hungry?" He ran his finger over the elastic band, back and forth. I couldn't think beyond the need for him to push the fabric aside and touch me. With his finger still tempting the edge of my panties, he brought his lips millimeters from mine.

"So, are you all wet and ready for me, Katherine?"

"Please..." I begged.

"You're gonna have to tell me what's waiting for me."

I wasn't a fool, "I'm drenched."

He ran his finger up, over the fabric, gently brushing it near but not on my clit.

"How long?" he asked.

I didn't answer. I was stubborn. I didn't want to give him the satisfaction of knowing that I liked him like this, possessive and animalistic. But I also needed him. I wanted him so badly that I was literally shaking with anticipation.

"Go on, tell me." He circled my nub of pleasure again. "How long have you been aching to feel my cock push inside you?"

"A while." I breathed. He pressed his erection, still trapped in his jeans, against my leg.

I begged again, "Oh, God, please..."

I don't know if I won or if his own need for pleasure overtook him, but he pushed my panties down and palmed my pussy. Then, he ran one finger straight up the middle until he was softly plucking at my clit, like I do my guitar.

I cried out my pleasure into the parking lot. If anyone was around, they heard me.

Shifting so he could use the hand that wasn't buried in my folds to unbuckle his pants, he growled again, "I'm gonna fuck you right here, Kat. In a goddamn parking lot. If that's not okay, you better speak up."

I didn't say a thing.

5

BILLY

S itting in the fast food joint, I suddenly saw it on her face, the yearning, the aching need. I knew Kat. I knew every breath, every expression, every tone of her voice, and in that moment, I knew my girl was horny. And not just a little bit. She was hard up and aching for me. And damn, if that knowledge didn't have me solid as a rock in seconds. Once we were outside, the way she trembled from the slightest touch of my fingertips... holy fuck, it was all I could do not to come in my Wranglers.

She might have been angry, but she liked the animal in me. It revved her engine so hard that she was about to let me take her against the door of my truck in a public parking lot. With my belt open, I pushed down my boxer briefs and freed my cock. I stroked myself once, watching her hungry eyes take in my girth. We were so close. She was still pinned against my truck. I liked her like this, wanton and waiting. Letting go of my cock, I grabbed her leg and wrapped it around my waist, pushing her jean skirt up and out of the way. Then, I used my hand to pull her panties to the side and situate my head at her opening. Kat was on the pill. She had been for a few years—nothing to do with us. There had never been anything between us and I liked it that way.

I hadn't lost sight of the fact that we were out in the open, on the verge of getting caught, but I couldn't help myself. I paused to listen to her beg. I loved hearing how much she wanted me and she didn't disappoint. She whined, "Please, Billy, do it now. I want to feel you."

Grabbing her ass and lifting her to me, I pumped my hips once, stopping when I was all the way in, when we were completely joined—no air between us. She whimpered, so fucking tight.

Rolling my hips but not pulling out, I growled, "This is mine."

She nodded fervently.

I pulled out and pumped in hard. "You are mine, Kat." I punctuated my statements with my fucking, "Do you understand that?" Driving and rocking, "No one touches you but me." Pushing and pulling, "This pussy is mine."

She was frenzied and crumbling, on the verge of going over the edge and coming hard, when she surprised me by saying, "Yes. Fuck. Oh, God, Yes, all yours. My pussy is yours."

I'd never heard her say pussy before. Let alone tell me hers was mine. I liked it. I liked it a lot. I drove harder, willing her to come all around me, "Tell me again, Kit-Kat. Tell me who commands this sweet little pussy of yours."

She was trembling but as she came, she cried out, "You do, Billy. You do."

That's all it took, I went over the edge with her on the word, "Mine."

We were both shuddered in the cool night air, quiet other than our panting breaths and the sound of my belt buckle jingling.

I kissed her, sloppy but sweet, touching her face with my hands. I still had her leg wrapped around my waist, but I pulled back enough so that I could see her eyes. I was a little worried that, post-orgasm, she might feel a little freaked out that we just fucked hard in public.

"You okay?" I breathed.

She smiled and bit her bottom lip, "More than okay."

Dropping my forehead to hers, I gushed, "I fucking love you."

She peppered my lips and cheeks with little kisses, "Me too."

Popping my head up and looking both ways, I teased, "What do you think? Should we get the hell out of here before someone calls the cops?"

She shrugged her shoulders and shifted to drop her foot to the ground, "My ass cheeks are starting to chill, so maybe."

I laughed as I tucked and buckled myself back into my clothes and she shimmied her skirt down. She turned to open the truck door and I pressed up against her, wrapping my arms around her torso, hugging her to me. She wrapped her arms around my arms, curling into me, making my heart soar.

"Billy?" she asked sweetly.

"Yeah, babe?"

"Did you just fuck me in a fast food parking lot?"

"Yeah, babe."

"Wow. So tacky, but so hot."

I could see it all in my mind, feel her, hear her. I couldn't help myself, I rutted against her tush. Shit. I broke away from our hug, stepping back, "We gotta go. Or it's gonna happen again."

With a wicked smile, she replied, "It's a long drive. There are a lot of burger joints between here and there."

6

KAT

A week after the show at Harry's and our flirt with exhibitionism, I was in my room working on a new song when my cell phone rang. It was a number I didn't recognize, so I'm not really even sure why I answered it. Usually, I would just dismiss an unknown caller as spam since they'll leave a message if they know me. But I was frustrated. I couldn't quite get the chorus of the song to work. Also, the sun was pouring through my window, making everything hot and sweaty. I don't know why, but I just acted strangely and answered the darned thing. My hands were full with my guitar and whatnot, so I put it on speaker.

A man's voice I'd never heard before said, "Is this Kat Bennett?"

Spam, I thought as I moved to hang up.

"Kat Bennett, who sang at Harry's Feeding Station last weekend?"

I backed my finger away from the red end call button. "This is Kat," I said.

"Oh, Kat!" the stranger's voice exclaimed. "I am so happy to talk to you. My name is Marcus Daily. I got your number from Laurie at Harry's, but you should know that she was really reluctant to give it to me."

Butterflies erupted in my stomach. Was this another gig? Or a fan? Or something creepy? No, not creepy. Laurie wouldn't give my number to a creep. "Can I ask why you're calling?"

"Oh, God, of course." He laughed to himself. "I'm a music manager."

I almost squealed.

He continued, "I was on vacation in Montana last week, skiing at Big Sky. Honestly, I wasn't looking for talent. I always check out local music when I travel. And as I'm sure you know, Harry's has a good reputation, so I stopped by. I saw your set. Really good stuff. I hung back to listen to the headliner, and by the time I went looking for you, well, you had left."

I was in a parking lot with Billy.

"Anyway, I figured that was that. But, here I am, a week later still humming your songs and, well, I would really like to manage you. Laurie told me you're a fresh face. Don't even have a demo. Is that right?"

What was happening right now? This was freaking crazy. "I'm sorry," I said, trying to sound calm. "Can you tell me a little bit more about you? You said you were on vacation, skiing in Big Sky. Where are you calling from?"

"New York."

My false bravado and the mask of calm dissolved instantly. I squeaked, "NEW YORK?"

He laughed. "Listen, Kat, I'm the real deal. You can look me up on the internet if you need to, Marcus Daily."

I should. I would. "I will," I said, trying to reclaim some semblance of contained excitement.

"What I'd like to do is fly you here, to New York, and record a demo. Maybe do some little gigs and see what kind of response we get."

"Okay." My voice was trembling and my hands were shaking. I put my guitar down on the bed and cradled my face in my hands for a second.

Marcus continued to explain, "Before we do that, I'm going to send you a management contract. Do you have a lawyer, Kat?"

I didn't respond. Holy crap, what was happening right now? How was I going to pay a lawyer?

"Are you still there?" Marcus asked.

I was. "Yes..." I paused, struggling to say anything and feeling totally overwhelmed. Finally, I said, "I don't have a lawyer. I'm not even sure I know a lawyer." I didn't tell him I wasn't sure I could afford one.

"Okay, well, I want you to get one. I want you to know that this is a real contract and that it's industry standard and no one's going to take you for a ride on my watch."

I smiled to myself, "You sound trustworthy," I offered.

"I am. But you don't know that yet. You want my first words of wisdom as your manager? If you're going to come out here to New York and make it in this business, you need to leave that small-town faith in humanity behind. This business is backstabbing and rough. It's not for the faint of heart. I'm not trying to scare you. You have the chops, but you're gonna need a thick skin."

I nodded and then realized he couldn't see me. "Got it," I said.

"Get a lawyer," he repeated. "Ask someone you trust to help you."

"I will." I was gonna ask Duke, Billy's dad. He'd know what to do.

"Okay, I'm going to transfer you to my assistant to get some details like your address, etc. I am really happy I wandered into Harry's, Kat. I think you are gonna make great music and I'm gonna make sure the world hears it."

Oh my God. "Thank you, Marcus," I said as sweetly as I could muster with so much elation trapped in my body just wanting to break free.

"Thank you, Kat."

After giving my address and personal details to Marcus's assistant, I hung up the phone and barreled down the stairs. I headed for the kitchen door, which was our back door and the most direct route to the Morgan's property. My momma was in the kitchen, sitting at the table drinking an ice tea. Our kitchen had looked the same for the last forty years. Avocado-colored appliances and yellow linoleum from the seventies. We didn't have the money to change it and, honestly, everything still worked so what was the difference?

"Where are you off to in such a hurry?" my mother asked. "You know those boys are still working." I had to tell a lot of people about what was happening to me, but there was only one person I really wanted to tell: Billy.

"I know, I know, I know." I was a buzz. "But I gotta talk to him."

"I'm sure it can wait a couple of hours, Kat. Don't bother them."

There was no way she was going to stop me. I had been leaning against the door, but I walked back to her. "Mama," I said. Kneeling on the floor in front of her and taking her hand in mine. "Something amazing just happened."

She smiled at me, a little haggard from her day waitressing at the local cafe, where I also took shifts.

"What? What fabulous thing happened now, beautiful girl?" she asked, lifting her hands to cradle my cheeks and bowing to kiss me on the forehead.

"A music manager from New York saw me at Harry's and he wants to sign me," I said, feeling giddy. My mother's eyes went as wide as flying saucers.

"What?" she squealed and jumped up, bringing her hands to cover her mouth like she was going to cry. I stood too, suddenly feeling guilty that I was rushing off to tell Billy. I was glad she stopped me and that I told her first. She pulled me into her arms and hugged me tight. With me pressed to her chest, she said, "It's happening. You're gonna be a star, baby."

I laughed.

When she finally let go, she said, "Go on. Go tell your blue-eyed cowboy."

I hugged her one more time and then I was running out the door. When I'd gotten about twenty feet away, I looked back and she was standing in the door frame behind the screen. I hollered, "I love you, mama. I love you so much."

7

BILLY

"Careful climbing that ladder, you two," I hollered after the twins, Cody and Sarah. They were escaping to the hay loft. Me and all my siblings were in the barn. My father had assigned us to everyone's least favorite task: stall mucking and overall barn care. Usually, on a Saturday, Luke, the eldest after me, and Wyatt, the monkey in the middle, would be out on the land checking the herds with my dad and the ranch hands he employed. But, we'd been particularly catty at the breakfast table. We were giving Luke a hard time because he doubled down on his ludicrous commitment to not eat cows (it's a long story). My father recently acquired some farm animals from a local farmer who needed to sell. Dad was a softy like that. So, we wound up with a few lambs and a coop of chickens, and now, Luke won't eat lamb or chickens either. Anyway, my dad got fed up with us. He's had a shorter fuse since our mama died. So, Wyatt and Luke got stuck on barn cleaning duty with me and our younger siblings.

Most Saturdays, I tended to Cody and Sarah. I was supposed to be teaching them how to run the ranch. Helping them master the basic skills. They already knew many things. Every Morgan child could ride a horse before they could reach a countertop. When I was their age, I could practically run the damn ranch, but since my mama died, our dad wasn't pushing Cody and Sarah the way he had Wyatt, Luke, and me. I think he felt that losing their mama so young was enough stress, no need to bury them in chores. That said, they were supposed to be helping us muck stalls, but honestly, I just didn't have the energy to corral them.

Wyatt also seemed to need to be corralled. Who was I kidding, Wyatt usually needed taming. As soon as we got to the barn, he'd jumped up on the thick edge of the stall we were mucking and cracked some book from his English class. Unlike the rest of us, Wyatt struggled in school. He wasn't stupid, but everything seemed harder for him. He always passed but just barely. It took him longer to do his school work than the rest of us and he was really sensitive about it. In all honesty, I wasn't sure if he was using his book to keep me from making him work or if he actually needed the extra time to get his work done. Wyatt was wily so you were never quite certain when you were being manipulated until it was all over and he'd gotten his way.

Luke and I bore the brunt of the work without complaint. We were used to picking up the slack for the others. Luke was the brother I was closest to and not just because we were closest in age. Luke, like me, was more serious than the others. I respected that. He was also somehow sensitive and strong and had this impenetrable honesty about him. Luke was incredibly loyal and he was funny without being unkind. I always enjoyed his company. Kat did too.

With a hard push of shovel into the muck, Luke said, "Hey, Bill, since you're old and all graduated now, I bet you didn't hear that little baby Wyatt played knight in shining armor this week?" That tiny dig at me being the oldest was a throw-away. Luke's goal with this comment was to get Wyatt's attention and ruffle his feathers. First of all, even at fourteen, there wasn't much little about Wyatt. By the time he was fully grown, Wyatt was going to be the biggest of us, and that was saying a lot because we were all burly. Secondly, Wyatt was not a knight-type. He was one hundred percent rogue, and he liked it that way.

I played along and raised the register of my voice so it was high-pitched like a gossipy lady, "Really? Do tell."

"Well, the way I heard it," Luke began, "Wyatt threw a fit at Mark Winston for bumping into Caroline Winchester."

This story was more interesting than I'd expected, "Sheriff Winchester's super smart, super off-limits daughter?"

Luke nodded.

"Well, that's interesting," I said, throwing a shovel full into the wheelbarrow we had between us.

Wyatt slammed his book shut and turned to us, infuriated, "Oh, come on. I wasn't going all white knight or whatever you two grandmas are gossiping about. It was rude. Mark freaking hip-checked her. Knocked her books out of her hands and made her trip. People were standing around laughing at her. It sucked. He's an ass."

Luke continued to poke the beast, "After Wyatt put Mark in his place, he helped Caroline gather her books and walked away with her."

"Really?" I exclaimed. Then, I turned to Wyatt. "And where did you get off to with the lovely Ms. Winchester?"

Wyatt rolled his eyes at me. "Oh, for heaven's sake. I took Caroline to her locker and I left her there. I'm not an idiot, y'all. She might be pretty under all that nerd, but that girl's brain is like a thousand times bigger than mine. Definitely way more than I could handle, and with the added trouble of her daddy... nope. No thank you." He reopened his book, signaling that he was done with us.

Luke turned to me, "Did you hear him say she was a hottie? Because that's what I heard."

I snickered, right before I heard Kat's voice, "Billy, Billy are you in here?" She usually left me to my work on Saturdays, so I was a little surprised, but she sounded more excited than frantic.

"We're over here," I hollered back.

As she approached, Wyatt put down his book again and Luke and I turned to face her. When she was finally standing in front of us, it was clear that she was beyond happy. Her eyes were bright and her smile was crazy wide. Her hair was in a messy ball on the top of her head and she was wearing old jeans, a navy-blue t-shirt, and no shoes. Whatever she was about to tell us was big, almost too big to contain. My ribcage started to feel like it was too small for my lungs.

I pointed to her feet, "Kat, you're in the barn without shoes."

She looked down, then looked up again, still beaming. "I guess I am."

I could tell that she wanted me to ask her what she was doing here or why she looked so happy, but I couldn't bring myself to do it. I knew that there were only two things in the world that made Kat this happy: me and music. Since I knew I hadn't done anything to elicit her glow, this was music-born, and that could go south for me, fast.

She bounced in place and then finally whined, "Come on, ask me why I'm here on a Saturday when I try not to distract you from your work on Saturdays?"

I still couldn't say anything. Out of the corner of my eye, I saw Luke looking at me, eyeing me up, waiting for me to say something, but he couldn't see that my bones had started to ache or that my stomach was in knots because I could see it all over her. This was the moment I'd been dreading.

After another beat, Luke stepped in for me, "Okay, I'll bite. What ya doing here, Kit-Kat?"

She turned to him, but not before concern quickly flashed in her eyes. She was squealing, but I could hear that her voice was a shade more somber when she said, "A manager from New York saw me at Harry's Feeding Station last weekend. He wants to sign me. He's flying me to New York to record a demo!"

There it was. Everything I'd been dreading. She was going to choose her music over me. She already had. She was gonna leave me and I couldn't stop her. First, my mom, now Kat. How was I going to breathe without her? I prayed for the ground under my feet to crack open and swallow me whole. It didn't.

Luke barreled towards her, picked her up, and spun her in his arms, hollering, "HOLY FUCK, KIT-KAT! That's amazing." High in the air, her face above Luke's head, Kat laughed, her eyes closed, her joy billowing through the barn like smoke.

Wyatt hopped down off the edge of the stall and headed for her too. He smacked into my side as he passed me, nodded his head towards Luke and Kat, and under his breath, whispered, "That's supposed to be you!"

I knew that, I did, but my feet were cemented to the ground.

From above us in the loft, Cody called out, "Why's Kat squealing like a piglet?" His tone was a touch bitter, like he couldn't bear other people's happiness. The harshness in his voice broke the spell of self-pity I was under. My mind jumped to another concern. Since our mom died, Cody had become a caustic little devil. He was a lot like Wyatt, only snarkier, angrier, and I was worried about him. And as much as I wanted Kat, Cody and Sarah were mine to worry about and care for. I promised our mama that I would make sure they grew up happy and loved. I wanted Kat here to help me do that, but it wasn't her job.

Before me, Luke put Kat down and Wyatt was hugging her now. Luke called up to Cody, "Kat's gonna be famous, little dude."

Suddenly, an equally squeaky Sarah flew over the loft edge and barreled down the ladder. Sarah was a musician like Kat. In fact, Kat taught her to play the guitar and they spent a lot of time writing music together. She reached the bottom of the ladder in record time and careened for Kat, wrapping her little arms around Kat's waist. She looked like a kid, wearing jeans, a hot pink t-shirt, an arm full of friendship bracelets, and teal Converse sneakers. She also still had a childish preteen voice, but looking up from Kat's armpit, Sarah fired off some very adult-like questions, "What happened? Did I hear you say manager? Is he sending a contract? Do you have a lawyer?"

Kat laughed again, kissing the top of Sarah's head. Then she said, "He is sending a contract and he did mention a lawyer." She shook her head, "I don't know one or how I'm gonna pay for it, but I'm gonna talk to your daddy and see if he can advise me."

I cleared my throat. Everyone turned to me. "I can pay for it," I said. A going-away present, I thought. "I have some money I've been saving up for you. For a demo."

Kat looked like she might cry. Sarah released her arms from around Kat's waist, and as if by instinct, Kat came to me. She hugged her arms around my torso and I kissed her, a sweet simple kiss. When our lips parted, she dropped her cheek to my chest.

"Thank you, Billy." Her voice was tender and full of love.

I wanted to say congratulations. But I was afraid that if I said anything else, she'd hear the dread in my voice.

8

KAT

I t was hot and it was late. It had to be after midnight. I had the fan on and the window open, but it was still sticky. Summer was coming, if it wasn't here already. I was supposed to be sleeping. My mama had tucked me in like I was five, kissed my forehead, and told me to get my beauty rest. She even looked back at me as she turned off the light and whispered, "Love you, baby girl." But I just couldn't sleep. A few days after Marcus called, I went to the lawyer with Duke. I signed the contract and paid with Billy's money. And now, in less than twelve hours, I was going to board the plane and head to New York, but instead of boiling over with nervous excitement, I felt panicked.

It was Billy. There was something off with him. After his weird non-reaction in the barn, he said and done all the right things. He gave me the money for the lawyer. He worried about what I would bring with me and where I would stay. He researched Marcus to see that he was legit. He asked a lot of questions and listened to the answers. Earlier tonight, he got his family to throw me a little celebration dinner. We laughed and talked and toasted like usual. Billy smiled and offered excitement when it was appropriate, but something wasn't right.

Since the moment in the barn when I told him and his siblings about Marcus's call, I felt like I was wandering around in a maze, trying to reach Billy. I could hear his voice and he was just right there, but there was this huge hedge between us. Every time I turned a corner, I'd hear him say, "I'm here," or I'd see a flash of him up ahead, but I just couldn't catch him. I couldn't look into his eyes and feel how he was wrapped around my heart.

Acting childish, like a middle schooler with a crush, I cornered Luke and drilled him about Billy's behavior. Honestly, I went full-on psycho girlfriend, but totally on the down-low. A few days after the barn incident, I was working one of my last shifts at the Conway Cafe. It was a Wednesday. Billy usually showed up for lunch during my shifts on Wednesdays. Since his mom, Molly, died, Wednesdays were the day of the week that Billy dedicated to running the household errands, with Duke's consent, of course. Anyway, he didn't show. By two-thirty, the cafe had all but cleared out and no Billy. Usually, if he wasn't gonna make it, he texted me or something. I called him, but he didn't answer. And then, I went full tilt in a matter of five seconds. He always answered my calls. I grabbed my mama's keys and barreled out the door, still in my uniform, still in the middle of my shift, with my mama hollering behind me, "Where are you going?"

Pedal to the metal in my mom's little beater Honda, I drove straight to the high school. I knew Luke would be in class until three-thirty but I didn't care. The building looked the same as it had a year ago when I graduated. A big old brick monstrosity that sat high on the roll of a little hill nestled in trees. It might have been a beautiful building, but sometime in the sixties or seventies, someone had decided to add a lot of metal awnings that made it look like a retro motel. I parked the car by the front circle, strode into the main office, and demanded that they call Luke out of class. Mrs. McCarthy, who had been the principal's office manager since my mother was a girl, was less than enthused. But I must have looked a little frazzled because she believed me when I said it was a family emergency.

"Do you need Wyatt as well, Miss Bennett?" she asked with clear and practiced diction.

"No, ma'am," I replied sternly. Then I snapped, "I'll wait outside. Please instruct him to meet me there."

She nodded, and as I strode back to the door, I heard her voice over the loudspeaker, "Luke Morgan, please come to the principal's office. Luke Morgan to the principal's office."

Outside, I leaned on the hood of my mama's car and let the sun and the spring air warm my skin. I took a few deep breaths, calming the anxiety in my chest. I told myself that I was being crazy, that I was just worked up from everything that was happening to me. Luke strolled out, calm and collected. He was a hard guy to ruffle, perhaps the most level-headed of the Morgan boys, but also the most creative and intuitive. He was the one I felt closest to besides Billy. His brothers gave him a lot of flak for being artistic and sensitive. They got a particular kick out of the fact that he was sort of a vegetarian. He looked different too. He had thick blonde hair that he kept long, even though Duke wished he would cut it. Honestly, I sometimes felt they were a little rough on him for having different interests and ideas, but he seemed to take it in his stride, so who was I to tell them differently?

When he got to me, Luke didn't ask a whole lot of questions, he just hugged me and then said, "It seems normal to be freaking out."

I loved that I didn't need to explain myself. He just got me. I asked, "He's being weird, right?"

He settled down next to me on the hood of the car. Then, he shrugged and confirmed, "A little."

I looked up at the sky all around us. It was so blue. I sighed, "He didn't come to the cafe for lunch today."

"He went out with dad this morning," Luke offered solemnly.

"He usually texts me when that's going to happen." I was quiet, feeling a little ridiculous but also sad.

"Maybe he forgot his phone," Luke suggested. He was also quiet.

"Maybe."

We stayed silent for a spell, sunning on the hood of my mama's car.

Eventually, Luke asked, "What'd you tell McCarthy to get her to send me out?"

"Just an emergency," I laughed.

"Musta looked right crazy for that old bat to do your bidding."

I smiled, closing my eyes and tilting my head back so it was more in the sun, "I'm a graduate now. She respects us more than you lowly pre-graduated peons."

He full-on guffawed before shaking his head, "Nope. No way. I'm betting you came in here all Cersei Lannister and she was afraid of you." Luke was a huge *Game of Thrones* fan.

"My Cersei is terrifying," I admitted.

"Damn straight," he agreed. Then, after a pause, he got serious and said, "I think he's just nervous."

"Yeah." I swallowed the word and ached a bit at the idea.

"And he's gonna miss you."

"It's only a week." I was whining, not because I was complaining, more because I hated the idea that he was hurting.

"He'll be okay," Luke said, no doubt in his voice. "I'll be here."

I nodded, almost crying but not sure why. I dropped my head to Luke's shoulder and rested there.

Luke was a good brother. Billy was lucky to have him. So was I. Talking to him settled my anxiety about Billy for the rest of the week, but tonight at dinner, the panic surged in my chest again. As usual, he sat next to me at the dining table, but he never rested his hand on my knee once. NOT ONCE. It wasn't that he never touched me. He did. He hugged me hello, put his arm around me when people were looking, but on any given day since the first time he kissed me, Billy Morgan's hand was under the dining table, creeping up my thigh to the point that I was always subtly slapping it away because it was straight up indecent to try to cop a feel in front of your whole family. But tonight, nada. Not one measly finger tickling my thigh. I didn't know what it meant, what was going on in his head, but I knew I didn't like it.

I couldn't leave it unsettled between us. So, even though he was the one taking me to the airport in the morning, I got up out of my bed as quietly as possible, tip-toed past my mama's room, and headed out the back door. I was still in my sleep shorts and a little lightweight tank top, no bra, no panties, but I wasn't planning on seeing anyone but Billy. And he'd seen me in less. I'd snuck into Billy's house before, more than once, but mostly when I was a little kid. He shared a room with Luke, so as we got older, my sneaking in was more about mischief than about sexy time. As teenagers, there was more sneaking into my house than his. But tonight wasn't about that. I just wanted to see him, talk to him, find out what was happening in that head of his.

As I got closer to his house, I noticed that there was light coming from the barn loft. Billy had a lantern up there. The barn loft was our spot. It was the place we'd gone to be alone together since we were kids. It was where we lost our virginities. It was where I held him after his mama died. It was the first place he told me he loved me. Whatever he was doing, he couldn't sleep either. As I got closer, I could hear "Hotel California" playing. I didn't alert him to my presence. I just went inside and climbed the ladder. He'd left the lantern just at the top, but I knew where he'd be—at the far end, sitting on a hay bale. They didn't actually need to use the loft for storing hay anymore. It was more a place for keeping tools and feed and other supplies, but Billy made sure there were still hay bales up there because they were functional for us and his siblings, great forts or play towers for Cody and Sarah, a place to hang for the others and when it was just us, walls of privacy.

He was where I expected him to be. He had the loft door pushed open a bit so that the stars could pour through. In the blue light of the moon, I saw that he was drinking one of Duke's beers. He'd pay for that later. Duke kept a tally of the alcohol in his house. I guessed that's what you did when you had five kids, especially when one of them was Wyatt. Billy was still dressed in the jeans and blue and white plaid shirt he'd worn to dinner, but he'd changed from his boots to a pair of flip flops. Watching his lips pull on the dark glass bottle made my throat feel tight. He wasn't a drinker. I took a step closer and the boards creaked under my feet.

He kept his eyes on the stars as he said, "I was just wishing you were here and now you are. Crazy, right?" His voice was low and hot like the air around us.

I crossed to him. Took the bottle from his hand, placed it on the floor next to the bale, and climbed onto his lap, straddling him. His breath smelled like beer, but I kissed him until he was sweet again. Through, the lightweight cotton of my little shorts, I felt him get hard beneath me, but he didn't immediately make any moves to drive us towards sex. He just held my face.

"I love you," he whispered. It wasn't unusual for him to tell me. He told me most days, but something about the tone seemed off—desperate and distant like he was saying goodbye.

I kissed him gently, trying to reassure him that everything was fine. "I love you too. More than the moon and the stars. More than anything."

"More than music?" he asked, his voice still laden with loss.

"Yes," I made sure there was no doubt in my voice. "More than music. More than everything." I couldn't imagine what he was picturing. Could he really think that, after growing up together and falling in love, I was going to go off, become a rockstar, and leave him behind? The notion was absolutely ludicrous to me, but I know that people can't control how they feel. Sometimes we can control how we respond to those feelings, but the feelings themselves are like wild animals, seemingly sweet one minute and deadly the next.

With determination and a show of strength, as if he needed to gain the upper hand, he picked me up and flipped us both so that I was lying on my back on the hay bale.

"I can't play. I need to be inside you," he said.

I nodded, confirming that I was his to have.

Quickly and efficiently, he removed his jeans and stripped my shorts from my body with such force that I worried they may have ripped and pictured myself walking home naked. Our kissing was enough to make me wet, but he spat on his hand anyway, stroking himself once just to be sure. And then, with my bare bottom crushing into the spiky odds and end of hay, he drove his cock deep into my pussy, again and again with a punishing rhythm. My heart and my mind knew that something about the way he was fucking me was ugly, brutal even. But when it came to passion, my body and pleasure were his to command. They had been since the first time his lips touched mine, maybe even before that. So,

I took what he was giving—the anger and the fear—and I welcomed it. He was my heart. If he was hurting, so was I. He didn't try to make eye contact or connect with my soul. He just took and I gave. When we came, our orgasms were hard and fast, loud and reckless.

When it was over, he collapsed against my chest, his brow sweaty, and I held him. He was quiet for a long time. I wished we were fully naked, his skin pressed to mine. The fabric between us seemed to function like a wall, keeping us apart. Needy for the feel of him, I ran my fingers through his thick brown hair. I listened to the sounds of the night, the shuffle of the horses below us, the chirp of crickets in the grass outside the barn, and the sedate hum of the world out there, somewhere, sleeping. With his face pressed into the fabric of my tank top, he said, "I love you."

A steady flow of quiet tears streaked my cheeks, "I know," I answered, sniffling a little. "And I love you too. Forever. I promise."

9

BILLY

I stood back while Kat hugged her mama, Miriam. Kat had already said goodbye to everyone in my family. Stuck watching it all, I couldn't seem to stay still. I'd checked the lock on the cargo box in my truck bed multiple times. I went back into Kat's house for a couple of bottles of water. I shifted in place when I should have been standing still. This big send-off only served to reinforce my feelings that I wasn't the only one who thought she'd be gone for more than a week. My dad looked downright teary-eyed when he hugged her, and he told her he was proud of her like a thousand times. Her mama was crying, a mixture of happy and sad tears.

We had to go before I lost my shit and drove off without her.

"Don't want you to miss your plane," I said.

"We're okay," Kat said, looking at her watch.

Miriam intervened, "No, no. He's right. You go on, baby." She shuffled Kat towards the passenger side of my truck and hugged her one more time. "I know you're gonna do great. You're gonna blow 'em away."

I was already behind the wheel. Kat climbed in the truck next to me, but her attention was still on her mama. Once the truck door was closed, smiling and bright, she called out, "I love you." The sound of her voice echoed around me, trapped in the cab of my truck. Then, she turned to all of my family, who were gravitating towards Miriam to encircle her with their care. Kat hollered at them, "Take good care of her for me!"

I will, I thought to myself, trying not to let the melancholy show. She waved and

blew kisses as I threw the truck into reverse and backed down the dirt driveway to the paved road a few hundred yards away, which my father had all but bought and paid for a couple of years back. I kept my head turned, looking out the back window, my right hand on Kat's headrest. It was warm for spring, but even in the height of summer, Montana's never so warm that you can't manage it. Even so, I felt sweaty. I'd made an effort to look my best. I wanted her to remember me as the cowboy that I was, clean-cut, but rugged and gruff, always in my hat and boots, always ready to ride.

Once their waving palms disappeared from view, she said, "I don't know what all this fuss is about. I'm only gonna be gone a week." She was deceiving herself. She didn't want to see what was so clear to me. She wasn't coming back anytime soon. When it came to music, Kat was irresistible. She might have a return ticket dated for a week from now, but that ticket would go to waste. A week would turn into a month, and then two months, and then she'd ask me to come and visit, and then in six months, she'd start wanting me to move there. Her music, her career, would become more and more important. She would choose her music. Maybe not intentionally, but it would happen. It already had. I couldn't bring myself to point it out. I couldn't tell her that she was leaving me today and that she wouldn't be back. I didn't want her to feel the end, yet. I didn't want to see the part of her that belonged to me dying. So, I tucked down all the feelings I let her see the night before and I put on a show.

"They're excited," I said. "We all love you. That's all." She examined my face, looking for a fracture in the mask I was presenting. I put my hand on her knee, "Come on, Kit-Kat, mind on the prize. You're going to New York today." With one more sweep of my face, she accepted my words as fact. And then we filled the space between Conway and Bozeman with meaningless conversation about things like what she should see and taste while she was in New York.

AT THE AIRPORT, I parked the car and walked her in. She'd printed her boarding pass, but we still waited in line to check her baggage.

"I don't know why I packed so much," she said, giving the large rolling bag in front of her a shove.

I did. Deep down, she wasn't sure when she'd be back. Honestly, if everything went the way she wanted, I wasn't sure she'd ever really be back. I smiled and shrugged. "You're a girl?" I suggested, pre-flinching for the smack the comment would illicit.

She didn't disappoint. "Sexist," she said, rolling her eyes and slapping me on the upper arm. With that behind us, she continued to lament her packing issues. "I just couldn't figure out what I was going to need, ya know? Marcus said not to worry because if there's something I need, I can get it there, but how? I mean, like with what money?"

"You have some money," I said. She did. She had about five hundred dollars that her mom and my dad gave her. 'Just in case' money.

"I don't think that's going to go very far in New York." She was nervous. I could hear it in her voice.

"I don't think you're going to pay for anything in New York."

She shrugged, "Maybe. But we don't know that." The check-in agent called for the next passenger, abruptly putting a stop to our conversation. The woman checking her in had long fake nails that were painted to look like a neon rainbow tie-dyed color. She asked for our boarding passes and I stepped back as Kat said, "I'm traveling alone."

They weren't for me but the words hit me like a punch to my gut. I literally almost buckled at the waist. She was traveling alone. My girl was leaving on a jet plane and I didn't know when she'd be back again. Fuck. I wanted to be the guy in the silly Hallmark movie, who steps up to the check-in clerk and says, *No, no, she's not traveling alone. I'm going with her.* But that wasn't an option for me. I had to take care of my family, and if I was being honest with myself, she didn't ask me to go with her. She never mentioned anything of the sort.

Boarding pass and luggage tag in hand, she stepped towards me and I threaded my fingers through hers. I was too overwhelmed to speak, so we walked to security in silence. We stopped about twenty feet from the security line. There were enough people waiting that dawdling too long didn't make sense. My heart was like a drum in my chest. She faced me and I lifted my hand and fingered a chunk of her auburn hair. It was shiny and glittered flecks of gold when the light hit it. Sometimes she still wore it in pigtails like Mary Ann from that old show, *Gilligan's Island.*

"Don't let anyone dye it," I said, not even sure what I was saying.

She laughed, "It's more likely I'd consent to a lobotomy." It was true. She thought of her red-headedness as part of her identity, but the Kat in front of me already felt unfamiliar, like when you see a photo of yourself doing something you have no memory of. It was like I couldn't find the emotional string that had always tied us together. My whole life it was as if we'd been linked with titanium, and now there was nothing but air between us.

She hugged me, sort of matter-of-factly, and then kissed me responsibly. "Back in a week," she said with a wink. "Promise."

I nodded. I kissed her again. "I love you," I said, my feet heavy like I had Mt. Rushmore in my boots.

"Me too," she said, stretching up on her tiptoes to sweetly kiss me one more time. Then, with a little bob of her head, she turned and headed for the TSA officer checking boarding passes.

When she was two feet from handing over her ticket, I freaked out. There was urgency in my voice when I called for her, "Kat."

She turned around instantly and ran back, jumping into my arms, her legs wrapping around my waist. I held her so tight that I worried she might be struggling to breathe.

In her ear, I whispered, "Come back to me."

"One week," she said and then I kissed her deeply, trying to affirm the imprint of my soul on her heart. When I let her go the second time, she walked backwards to the TSA officer and handed him her boarding pass with her eyes still locked on mine.

"I love you," she mouthed as he handed her back her ticket.

I nodded. "Me too."

I watched her each step of the way, showing her license, x-raying her purse, walking through the metal detector. She watched me too.

Once she was through security, standing on the other side of all the ropes and machines and official-looking employees, she stopped, just for me. She lifted her hand and waved. She was wearing black leggings, caramel-colored boots, and a loose white sweater. She smiled weakly. Maybe it was my fear, but I thought she looked sad, sadder than a week implied.

I lifted my hand and waved too. And then I watched her walk away.

They liked me. Before I could say boo, the demo was converted into an album. On the sly, Marcus invited a few people to listen to me in the recording studio. He didn't even tell me. By the end of that first week, I was signed by one of the big four recording companies, LSA Records. I got lucky beyond belief with Marcus. I have to admit, he wasn't a warm and fuzzy guy, but he was honest with me every step of the way, and he took care of me and respected my process as an artist. He promised me that no one would have control of my music but me, and he'd negotiated a contract that gave me creative freedoms and total control, something that just doesn't happen for newbie musicians. Also, I was sort of rich. I mean, for me I was rich. I got a $300,000 advance. That's a lot of money to a girl who is used to making nine dollars an hour. Also, Marcus explained that if my album sold, I was going to be really rich, like the kind of rich I didn't under-stand, like private planes and multiple houses rich.

New York was a lot.

I mean, it was exciting, but it was also a lot. And New York was big and all the buildings were so tall. From the minute I got off the plane, I felt out of my element. It was dirty and loud and it was hard to see more than a square of sky at any one time. There were good things about it too. I had Vietnamese food for the first time and it was amazing, like a flavor parade in your mouth—sweet, spicy, and tangy all at once. Also, New York pizza was just better. It was ooey and gooey, and crispy and salty. I couldn't get enough of it. Anytime anyone asked me what I wanted to eat, I said, "Pizza," and everyone laughed.

The people who were working with me were incredible. On day one, I'd gone from being the girl with no demo to the girl working on an album with Josh Devrow, the producer who helped create two of the last five albums of the year and something he worked on was nominated every year. His work crossed the lines of country and pop so we were a perfect fit. He was also funny and warm and didn't make me feel pressured or naive, and he was all about my music. Josh was one of the lynch pins in my record deal. He and Marcus were friends. They had been for years. So, Marcus had Josh in the studio with me the day I arrived. He wasn't my producer yet, but Marcus also had never asked Josh to come and see one of his clients, so he didn't arrive begrudgingly.

He came in with a smile on his face. He was handsome, not like Billy was, but tall and fit with hair so dark it made me think of Snow White. He had an air about him that commanded respect. Marcus mentioned that someone was coming to hear me sing, but he didn't tell me who. Producers aren't necessarily famous, I didn't know him on sight. When he came into the control room, I was sitting in one of the chairs in front of the board, tuning my guitar, preparing to go into the live room—the part of the studio with the mics and what not—and sing. He settled down on the couch, crossed his legs, so his ankle was resting on his knee, and said, "Okay, let me hear it."

I looked to Marcus for direction. He lifted his chin as if to say, "Go on, play." The guy didn't even introduce himself. I put my guitar down. Stood, stuck out my hand, and with a little haut in my voice, said, "Hi, I'm Kat Bennett, and you are?"

Josh laughed. Marcus did too.

"Told you. She's not mired in the shit of this business," Marcus said.

Josh stood and crossed to me, "Josh Devrow."

I'm sure he saw the flash of recognition cross my gaze, but I was a cowgirl, raised heartily. I wasn't gonna get scared or flustered just because he had talent. "Nice to meet you, Josh. I'm a fan. Your work is good."

He smiled, returned to his position on the couch, and only then said, "Let's see if I feel the same about you."

I didn't flinch. I just sat down, picked up my guitar, finished tuning, and played. I sang a sweet upbeat love song. One I'd written when I was fifteen, wishing Billy would just kiss me already. It was called *Waiting on You*. It was the kind of song that made people happy, a smiley, bright song. The kind of song you sing in the shower or the car when you're feeling good.

Josh watched me with a vivid intensity. He leaned in, resting his elbows on his knees. He was like a superhero calling on his heightened senses. First, his eyes focused hard, watching my fingers on the strings, then he closed his eyes and turned his head so his right ear was facing me, taking in every nuance of my tone. When I was done, he didn't say anything about the song or me. He just asked, "You got another one? Something sad this time?"

I didn't answer. I just started playing. This time, a song I wrote when I was twelve, a song about not knowing my father, called *Do I Have Your Eyes?* It was a slow ballad, dripping in the certain loneliness that an abandoned child feels, a real crooner. Josh continued to study me. It should have been unnerving, but he didn't seem to be finding flaws in my performance. He was just probing it.

When I finished the sad one, he asked for one more, "What if I want to dance?"

I could do that too. I played most of my gigs in a local cowboy bar. Cowboys liked to be swept off their feet. I chose a song called *Can't Catch Me*. To a stranger, it sounded like it was about a woman avoiding men's advances, but it was actually inspired by watching all four Morgan boys try to catch a calf that just didn't want to get caught. Billy laughed every time I sang it.

Halfway through the song, Josh leaned back and let his ankle tap out the rhythm as I sang. When I finished, he smiled and repeated my words back to me, "I'm a fan. Your work is good."

He signed on that day, even before I had the record deal in place. I heard him tell Marcus that I had the goods and that he'd clear his schedule for me. Honestly, I was pretty sure it was all a dream and I would wake up any minute.

That first night, back in my hotel, high on the idea that Josh was going to produce me, I called Billy. I was lying on the king size bed in a hotel room that felt fancy and unfamiliar, all this crazy stuff was happening for me and I missed him.

"I wish you were here," I said.

"Sarah and Cody need me," he said almost sternly, which felt like a strange response to my missing him. I wasn't trying to make him feel guilty. I just loved him. He picked up on his own tension, "Sorry, it was a long day here. Ignore me. How was your first day? Is the hotel okay?" They were perfunctory questions. He was actively trying to make space for me to talk about myself. He did this when he was stressed. It was part of how he loved me, setting his worries aside to make my life a priority.

I complied, "Josh Devrow listened to me play today."

"Who's that?" he asked.

I laughed. "Only like the most important music producer of the last five years. He's got Grammys and makes albums that sell millions.

"Wow," he said but he didn't sound excited. He almost sounded sad.

"He liked me. He's gonna produce my album. I don't think it's a demo anymore. I can't believe I've only been here a day."

"That's awesome, Kat." Again, his tone was off. Instead of exuberance, he was giving off something akin to sarcasm. "Listen, I'm sorry, babe. I'm exhausted. Can we talk about all this tomorrow?"

I felt angry but I didn't let it show, "Yep. Get some rest."

"Night," he said. And then he was gone.

AFTER THAT FIRST DAY, everything moved quickly. The second day brought the record deal and then I was in the studio with Josh, Marcus, and some truly incredible musicians for sixteen hours a day. I always texted Billy but sometimes there was no time to talk. The music was extraordinary. I was proud of what I was doing. The Saturday night before I was supposed to fly home, I called Billy to let him know that I thought it was going to be another couple of weeks. As soon as the demo became an album, I figured he would have understood that a week was not enough. It was late in New York, almost midnight, and I was once again lying alone in my big hotel bed. I was up early, before six, so I was tired.

When he answered the phone, it sounded like he was out.

"Where are you?" I asked.

"Sadie's," he answered. "Can you speak up? I can hardly hear you."

"I just wanted to tell you that I'm not coming home tomorrow. I mean, I figured you knew that but we never actually discussed it."

"Yep," he said, his voice like ice.

"I think it'll be a couple more weeks."

He spoke to the bartender, not me, and his voice was downright cheery, "Hey, Rose, can I get a coke?"

"You sound busy. I guess I should let you go."

"Yeah, lots going on here in little old Conway." Sarcasm, for sure.

"I'll call tomorrow."

"You do that," he said and then he was gone again.

He was mad. It was totally unreasonable. His mad made me mad. I punched both my arms into the bed I was lying on and made an exasperated sound. I couldn't understand why he was doing this to me right now. I understood that he had to be at the ranch and that he couldn't leave his family. But why couldn't he understand that I had to be in New York? Why couldn't he be happy for me? What was going on with him?

I was tempted to drop everything and fly home. I was. But you don't walk away from what was happening to me. You grab an opportunity like the one Marcus offered me by the reins and you ride. That's the only choice. When this was all over and I got back to him, Billy would understand why I had to stay. I knew he would.

ON SUNDAY, we took the day off. I didn't want to. I wanted to get this album done and get back to Conway, but I had to respect that not everyone had my drive to finish and some of the musicians had family. It wouldn't be fair to ask everyone to work seven days a week. Marcus tried to manage my day, offering to meet me or hire a tour guide to show me around, but I convinced him I just wanted some time to wander. I went for a walk, bought a croissant at a little French bakery, and ate it sitting on a rock in Central Park. It was warm but there was still a cool breeze. I tilted my face into the sun and let the rays warm me like I was a lizard or a lazy cat. Being far away from Billy was so uncomfortable and feeling emotionally distant from him was unbearable. I wanted to talk to him. I wanted to gush about all the good that was happening to me and lament that he wasn't by my side. When I agreed to come to New York, I thought he'd be with me in spirit. I thought I'd be doing things like FaceTiming him to show him the studio or sending him pictures of pizza and croissants. But instead, I dreaded our phone calls.

Every time we spoke, he made me upset. If I didn't feel angry because he was being a jerk, I felt guilty because something good was happening to me and he was excluded from my success. We were a mess. And I didn't want to be a mess. I didn't want to be mired in the drama of my relationship. I wanted to enjoy the moment. I wanted to experience the day as Kat Bennett, newly discovered but quickly skyrocketing musical talent. I wanted to wander around New York City and take in the sights. I wanted to talk to strangers on the steps of the Metropolitan Museum and go to the top of the Empire State Building. I wanted to see the night sky on the ceiling of Grand Central Station and eat a pretzel or a hot dog from a street vendor. I wanted to be someone other than the girl who was breaking her lover's heart because her own dream came true.

So, I didn't call. I let the day go by and I didn't call.

Instead, I went to the Guggenheim. Honestly, I'd seen art before but I'd never been to an art museum of that caliber. I spent hours wandering from one room to the next. I climbed up and down the circular ramp more than once just in awe of the architecture alone. I was amazed by how the space was used to accentuate the exhibitions, that the museum's curators actually used the rotunda in a theatrical way, asking onlookers to stand at the edge of the ramp and look down to experience both art and performance. I stood in front of a painting by Hilma af Klint, which looked like pastel and citrus-colored orbs to me. It was as large as the king size bed in my hotel room and I wondered how a person conceives of something so enormous, let alone the practicalities of painting such things. How do you paint the middle of a painting that you can't reach by standing at the edge? Ladders? An intricate pulley system?

When I left the park and walked to the Guggenheim, I thought I'd take a peek and then move on to explore some other parts of the city, but I was in the museum for most of the afternoon. There were so many things I didn't understand, things I didn't know. There was an entire world that I had never explored. Each new thing felt like adding a layer to the cake that was my mind. Alone in the museum, I realized that I'd been adding layers since I boarded the plane to New York and that these were the first layers of my life where Billy wasn't part of the recipe. Feeling hollow inside, I walked out on to the curb and walked 5th Avenue down to the Plaza Hotel. The weather was perfect and the city was milling with life. New York was loud. The hum of the city was honky and screamy and yet, somehow, it felt extremely isolating. I sat next to the Pulitzer Fountain in the little park in front of the historic hotel and watched the people, women pushing strollers, men in top hats hawking horse-drawn carriage rides, and construction workers eating food. The world was bigger and more complicated than I'd ever imagined but I wasn't sure that any of it really mattered to me. If I couldn't share this big new world with Billy, then did I really care what kind of world it would be?

My heart longed for the cool musk of the Morgan's barn loft, the smell of the hay, the rustle of the horses, and Billy's arms around me. If music didn't burn under my skin like an all-consuming fire, then I would happily be there, rolling in the hay with my cowboy. I had to get home. Not today. But soon. I pulled my phone out of my pocket and dialed his number. It rang but he didn't pick up. I called again. I felt crazed like if I didn't tell him I loved him right then, I might never get to say the words again. The phone rang again.

He picked up this time.

"What?" That was how he answered, blistery.

"I..." I was taken aback by how angry his voice sounded.

He huffed out a sigh, "What do you need, Kat? I'm busy."

I tried not to cry.

"We hadn't spoken today. I just wanted..."

He laughed sardonically, "Because you didn't call. I know you have this big new life in the big city, but today was your day off, right?"

"Yes," I said quietly because I was guilty that I'd avoided calling.

"You promised me you'd come back in a week and you didn't. And then you had a day off and you didn't want to talk to me. Honestly, I don't really want to talk to you right now."

"I miss you all the time..." I said.

He picked up that there was more to be said, "But..."

"But I have to be here now. I can't help that."

"You could. You choose not to. You could be here with me."

I paced in front of the Pulitzer Fountain and all the New Yorkers passing by paid no attention to my agitated state. "Billy, you know that I can't come home now. You're being unreasonable." My voice shook and I spat the words at him through the phone.

"You're right, I am." He wasn't conceding. "I know that. But I also know that I need you and you're not here. And honestly, Kat, you're not gonna be here. You're gonna be recording and then promoting and then touring. And then there will be another album." He was so angry that he'd stopped screaming. Instead, his voice was cold and withdrawn. "I don't think you'll ever really be back. And the thing is, I don't think I'm ever leaving."

I was crying now on a street corner in the sun. "Please stop," I begged.

But he didn't, "The choice is yours, Kit-Kat. Music or me?"

I was stunned. I was also red hot and angry. "No," I growled.

"No?" he responded incredulously.

"I will not let you do this," I said each word with intention. "We love each other for a lifetime. We can figure this out. It's not a choice I'm willing to make. We can have everything. You just need to be patient."

Now his voice was solemn, "I hear what you're choosing, Kit-Kat. And I hope it turns out to be everything you ever wanted."

"Please stop. I love you."

"Me too," he said. And then he hung up.

———————

THREE WEEKS LATER, Billy still hadn't spoken to me. He didn't answer my calls or texts. He wouldn't explain himself to Luke or Duke or anyone else. He was just gone. When I finished the album, I considered flying home, but it wouldn't change anything because, even if I did, I'd still be coming back. He was right that there were engagements for promotion and a tour. My life was a high-speed train. I could have made room for him in it, but I couldn't be the girl who lived a stone's throw from his barn anymore. I didn't fully understand why the situation wasn't an option for him, but he'd made it clear that he wasn't going to take the time to explain it any further. And the truth was, as each day passed, I got angrier. Before there was nothing left to say, I wrote him a letter:

DEAR BILLY,

It's been three weeks since I heard your voice. I feel like I'm starting

to forget the sound of you. I'm angry. I feel like you are being so selfish and

like I didn't mean nearly as much to you as you meant to me. How can you

just throw away everything we had? How could you love me one day and dispose of me the next? Am I just trash to you?

I don't know myself without you. It's hard to breathe. I keep thinking

that we are like the teeth on a zipper. Without both sides, the zipper doesn't

work. And then I remember that you don't call and you don't write and you

don't care that you have taken this dream of mine, this thing that I've wanted to

do every day of our entire lives, this thing that should have felt like a magical

whirlwind for me, and you've made it a nightmare. Did you want me to hate

you? Did you push me away because you thought I'd be better off? Is that

a thing people only do to each other in the movies? In my life, the only two

men who were supposed to love me didn't love me enough to stay. What

does that say about me?

I can't imagine that I'll never touch you again, never hold your hand,

never kiss your face. You pretended to give me a choice—but really, you

chose for me. I'm not coming back to Conway. I'm not coming back to you because you've shown me that there is nothing to come back to. So, I guess

it's time to harden my heart. I'm writing this letter to say good-bye, my love.

May the wind be at your back,

Kat

I SEALED THE LETTER IMMEDIATELY, addressed it, stood, and took it downstairs to the lobby of the hotel that I had started to call home. Tomorrow, I was going to look for an apartment. The concierge recognized me. He was a young guy in his twenties. I'd gotten his advice often in the last month. We talked a bit about some things. I knew he wanted to be on Broadway and that he'd been dancing since he was three.

"Good evening, Miss Bennett. How can I help you today?" he asked.

I handed him the letter. "Would you mail this for me?" I asked, working hard to get the words out without falling apart.

"My pleasure," he said. Then, after a pause, he asked, "Is there anything else? Perhaps cookies or some ice cream?"

I smiled half-heartedly, "That obvious?"

He shrugged, then dropped the professional pretense, "Heartbreak sucks. If there is anything I can do, let me know."

I nodded and turned back toward the elevators.

There was nothing to be done. Billy and Kat, fated, inseparable from the start, that was over. I would never be the same. When I got back to my room, I ran a bath but I never actually got in. I just sat on the edge of the tub and cried.

I would always love him.

In my heart, he would always be mine.

To Be Continued...

Want more Kat, Billy, and the rest of the Big Sky Boys?

LINK TO PURCHASE

HER COMEBACK

PART 2

1

KAT

Ten Years Later...

THERE WAS NOWHERE in the world that made my heart sing like Montana. The way the grassy knolls rolled into sharp snowcapped mountains that seemed to lord over and protect the docile valleys, the way it felt like you could reach out and touch the deep blue sky, the way the air reminded you of dipping your bare feet in ice-cold river beds, it was and always would be the only place that felt like home to me. And still, I hadn't planned on ever coming home again.

The day was unfolding easier than I had expected. Somehow, I'd traipsed a *Rolling Stone* reporter through my hometown of Conway, Montana without running into anyone worth a damn—and by that, I mean without accidentally bumping into anyone who made me think of Billy Morgan. As reporters go, Casey Stevens was perfectly lovely but still nosey. I mean, that's her job after all, but I didn't want to talk about Billy Morgan. We'd been to Sadie's, the town bar and the first place I got paid to sing. We'd met Mr. Lewis who taught me to play the guitar and Mrs. Turner who made me go to summer school for Biology, and now we were in the car with my entourage on our way to the Conway Cafe to chat up Hazel, who was the riskiest visit. Hazel owned the cafe. I worked there all four years of high school. She knew me better than the rest, so Billy might come up.

Casey had been quiet on the drive so far. I looked out the car window, hoping I appeared nostalgic. But really, I just didn't want to talk. Not about Billy or the many other topics I wanted to avoid. For example, my father, who didn't love me enough to stick around, my dating life for the last decade, which was as brutal as a four-car pile-up on the highway, my writer's block, I hadn't written anything in months, or my crappy last record. This visit to Conway was not by choice. After my third album was panned, Marcus, my manager, and my PR team decided that before I took a stab at the next album, my fans needed to remember I was a small-town girl. So, here I was back in the town I hoped to forget, surrounded by everything that reminded me of the worst heartbreak I'd ever known.

"Where did you live?" Casey suddenly asked. "Are we going to see your old house?"

Marcus answered from the front seat without ever looking up from his phone, "When the first album went platinum, Kat moved her mom to New York so they could be close and sold the house she grew up in to the neighbors."

What Marcus didn't say was that the neighbors were the Morgan's—Billy's family.

"Great. When are we going there?" Casey asked.

I kept my answer vague, "They're busy folks. Run a ranch. They bought it for the grazing land. I'd be surprised if it's even still there."

"We could drive by ..." Casey suggested.

"Yeah, maybe," I threw her a bone to put her off the scent. "If Hazel doesn't talk your ear off first. We need to make sure we get back to my plane at a decent hour. It's starting to look like it might storm."

Casey looked down at her pad of notes. Then she said, "Tell me about the first album."

I didn't want to talk about the first album at all. It was the album that I wrote before I left. It was the album of a lovesick fool. "Sure, what do you want to know?"

"Um ..." she flipped through her yellow notepad, landed on the page she was looking for, and said, "Who is *Blue Eyed Beau* about? Was that based on someone you knew here in Conway?"

For years, I'd been PR trained for moments like this. "I mean, yeah. It was about a local boy, but honestly, no one to speak of. Just a high school crush." I pointed ahead through the front window, "The Conway Cafe is just up here to the left."

The street was pretty empty in the late afternoon, so the driver parked the black SUV right in front. Marcus, Casey, my assistant, June, and I piled out onto the curb, and for a second, I felt like an asshole. I mean, in New York, being famous, being a rockstar was normal. It was normal to have all of these people with me all of the time. It was normal to have some guy in a suit driving me around. In Conway, it felt like I thought I was important.

My hometown might as well have been called Small Town, USA. Conway had a lot of land. They call Montana big sky country for a reason. There was a lot of sky over big fields. It was ranch country through and through. I mean, we had a Wal-Mart, but basically, we were still a homespun kind of place. Everyone knew everyone. Our main street was tree-lined. Our town Santa Claus was Mr. Parker, and one day, it would be Mr. Parker's son if it wasn't already. There was one beauty shop, one pizza place, and an ice cream stand that was only open April through September. For most Conway residents, cappuccinos were still "fandangled coffees" for urban people, at least they were when I left.

Immobilized by my encounter with my past, I stood on the curb looking left and right. A young woman I didn't know crossed the street. She didn't look like the Conway I remembered at all. She was pretty, but she wasn't homespun. She looked almost punky, like I could have seen her on a corner in Brooklyn. Her hair was bright blue. She had huge doe eyes and a curvy figure. She smiled as she passed us and then did that thing that people do when they pass a celebrity. She slowly looked back with narrowed eyes, clearly wondering to herself, *is that Kat Bennett?*

I put on my sunglasses and headed for the cafe door. Hazel had me in her arms before I even stepped through the door. "Sweet baby Jane, well aren't you a sight for sore eyes."

I was caught off guard by the tightness in my chest and the tears in my eyes. I hadn't realized I missed her.

Hazel leaned back, holding me at arm's length, and inspected my face, "Pie, you need pie. You look tired and underfed. Don't they feed you out east?"

She turned and started moving toward the counter, calling out behind her, "Kat always loved a warm slice of my strawberry rhubarb. I'm fetching the rest of y'all apple unless you speak up."

Never one to miss the opportunity to assert his opinion, Marcus said, "I actually prefer crumb cake."

I could feel June shaking her head behind me, as she said, "Thank you, ma'am."

I took a seat on one of the red stools. The Conway Cafe was exactly as you'd imagine it. A soda shop counter in a large room filled with rickety wood round tables and a mix and match collection of chairs. There was no particular color scheme, but the place was homey. And it smelled like heaven. That is, if your version of heaven is forty some odd years of pie.

Hazel looked older. She was letting her hair go gray. She had to be nearing her sixties by now. She was round, but she was always round. I mean, the woman makes pies for a living.

After slicing pie and crumb cake and making sure everyone had a fork, Hazel looked at me and said, "Well, I was pretty sure I was never going to see you again, so what brings you back?"

Selling a PR tour to Hazel felt insincere. "Casey here," I pointed to her, "is a reporter for *Rolling Stone* magazine."

"Oh, so it's a show and tell?" There was sarcasm in her tone, but she was smiling.

Casey didn't miss a beat. She leaned in and asked, "What did you bring to show and tell, Hazel?"

"I got stories, kid. But, we're old school around here. If it ain't mine to tell, I'm not telling."

"Well, what *can* you tell me, Hazel?" Casey smiled, leaning back on her stool.

Hazel took a deep breath, "She was a good kid, talented. We all knew that she was something special right from the start. I was standing right here with her mom the first time we heard her song on the radio. Kat's momma worked here too. The restaurant was full. It was lunchtime and everyone put their forks down. Everyone in town is a Kat Bennett fan and has been since she was a girl, so hearing her voice come through the radio just about knocked our socks off. When the song was through, the whole place broke into applause and people started hugging and kissing Kat's momma. Her name's Miriam, by the way, Kat's momma."

I blushed, I'd heard that story before but it made me feel happy. I turned to Casey,

"My mom and Hazel are friends."

"And now your mom lives in New York, with you?" We'd covered this ground earlier, but it was a conversation I didn't mind having so we could hang out here all day. "Yes. As soon as I could, I brought her to me. We're close, and I like having her nearby. Every now and then, she comes back here to visit. With touring and recording, it was just too hard to ..."

I was interrupted by the jingling bell on the cafe door. A hulk of a man walked in, hollering, "Heeeeeyzeeeel!" He was almost singing the word. "We need pie. What do you have in store for us today, you sweet ray of sunshine?"

When he caught sight of me, the hunky cowboy dead stopped with a stunned look on his face. It took me a second. When I left Conway, this hulk of a man was a pimply-faced fourteen-year-old kid. This was Wyatt Morgan. One of Billy's little brothers.

Behind Wyatt, another man came in, he must have been looking down at his phone. All I could see was the tipping brim of his hat. He said, "She's asking for cherry," right before he ran smack dab into Wyatt's back. "What the heck, Wyatt?"

He couldn't see me, and I couldn't see him. But I knew his voice better than my own: Billy Morgan.

2

KAT

There was nowhere in the world that made my heart sing like Montana. The way the grassy knolls rolled into snowcapped sharp mountains that seemed to lord over and protect the docile valleys, the way it felt like you could reach out and touch the deep blue sky, the way the air reminded you of dipping your bare feet in ice-cold river beds, it was and always would be the only place that felt like home to me. And still, I hadn't planned on ever coming home again.

The day was unfolding easier than I had expected. Somehow, I'd traipsed a *Rolling Stone* reporter through my hometown of Conway, Montana, without running into anyone worth a damn—and by that, I mean without accidentally bumping into anyone who made me think of Billy Morgan. As reporters go, Casey Stevens was perfectly lovely but still nosy. I mean, that's her job after all, but I didn't want to talk about Billy Morgan. We'd been to Sadie's, the town bar and the first place I got paid to sing. We'd met Mr. Lewis who taught me to play the guitar and Mrs. Turner who made me go to summer school for biology, and now we were in the car with my entourage on our way to the Conway Cafe to chat up Hazel, who was the riskiest visit. Hazel owned the cafe. I worked there all four years of high school. She knew me better than the rest, so Billy might come up.

Casey had been quiet on the drive so far. I looked out the car window, hoping I appeared nostalgic. But really, I just didn't want to talk. Not about Billy or the many other topics I wanted to avoid. For example, my father, who didn't love me enough to stick around; my dating life for the last decade, which was as brutal as a four-car pile-up on the highway; my writer's block because I hadn't written anything in months; or my crappy last record. This visit to Conway was not by choice. After my third album was panned, Marcus, my manager, and my PR team decided that before I took a stab at the next album, my fans needed to remember I was a small-town girl. So, here I was back in the town I hoped to forget, surrounded by everything that reminded me of the worst heartbreak I'd ever known.

"Where did you live?" Casey suddenly asked. "Are we going to see your old house?"

Marcus answered from the front seat without ever looking up from his phone. "When the first album went platinum, Kat moved her mom to New York so they could be close and sold the house she grew up in to the neighbors."

What Marcus didn't say was that the neighbors were the Morgans—Billy's family.

"Great. When are we going there?" Casey asked.

I kept my answer vague. "They're busy folks. Run a ranch. They bought it for the grazing land. I'd be surprised if it's even still there."

"We could drive by..." Casey suggested.

"Yeah, maybe." I threw her a bone to put her off the scent. "If Hazel doesn't talk your ear off first. We need to make sure we get back to my plane at a decent hour. It's starting to look like it might storm."

Casey looked down at her pad of notes. Then she said, "Tell me about the first album."

I didn't want to talk about the first album at all. It was the album that I wrote before I left. It was the album of a lovesick fool. "Sure, what do you want to know?"

"Um..." She flipped through her yellow notepad, landed on the page she was looking for, and said, "Who is 'Blue Eyed Beau' about? Was that based on someone you knew here in Conway?"

For years, I'd been PR trained for moments like this. "I mean, yeah. It was about a local boy, but honestly, no one to speak of. Just a high school crush." I pointed ahead through the front window. "The Conway Cafe is just up here to the left."

The street was pretty empty in the late afternoon, so the driver parked the black SUV right in front. Marcus, Casey, my assistant, June, and I piled out onto the curb, and for a second, I felt like an asshole. I mean, in New York, being famous, being a rock star was normal. It was normal to have all of these people with me all of the time. It was normal to have some guy in a suit driving me around. In Conway, it felt like I thought I was important.

My hometown might as well have been called Small Town, USA. Conway had a lot of land. They call Montana big sky country for a reason. There was a lot of sky over big fields. It was ranch country through and through. I mean, we had a Wal-Mart, but basically, we were still a homespun kind of place. Everyone knew everyone. Our main street was tree-lined. Our town Santa Claus was Mr. Parker, and one day, it would be Mr. Parker's son if it wasn't already. There was one beauty shop, one pizza place, and an ice cream stand that was only open April through September. For most Conway residents, cappuccinos were still "fandangled coffees" for urban people, or at least they were when I left.

Immobilized by my encounter with my past, I stood on the curb looking left and right. A young woman I didn't know crossed the street. She didn't look like the Conway I remembered at all. She was pretty, but she wasn't homespun. She looked almost punky, like I could have seen her on a corner in Brooklyn. Her hair was bright blue. She had huge doe eyes and a curvy figure. She smiled as she passed us and then did that thing that people do when they pass a celebrity. She slowly looked back with narrowed eyes, clearly wondering to herself, *is that Kat Bennett?*

I put on my sunglasses and headed for the cafe door. Hazel had me in her arms before I even stepped through the door. "Sweet baby Jane, well, aren't you a sight for sore eyes."

I was caught off guard by the tightness in my chest and the tears in my eyes. I hadn't realized I missed her.

Hazel leaned back, holding me at arm's length, and inspected my face. "Pie, you need pie. You look tired and underfed. Do they feed you out east?"

She turned and started moving toward the counter, calling out behind her, "Kat always loved a warm slice of my strawberry rhubarb. I'm fetching the rest of y'all apple unless you speak up."

Never one to miss the opportunity to assert his opinion, Marcus said, "I actually prefer crumb cake."

I could feel June shaking her head behind me, as she said, "Thank you, ma'am."

I took a seat on one of the red stools. The Conway Cafe was exactly as you'd imagine it. A soda shop counter in a large room filled with rickety wood round tables and a mix and match collection of chairs. There was no particular color scheme, but the place was homey. And it smelled like heaven. That is, if your version of heaven is forty some odd years of pie.

Hazel looked older. She was letting her hair go gray. She had to be nearing her sixties by now. She was round, but she was always round. I mean, the woman makes pies for a living.

After slicing pie and crumb cake and making sure everyone had a fork, Hazel looked at me and said, "Well, I was pretty sure I was never going to see you again, so what brings you back?"

Selling a PR tour to Hazel felt insincere. "Casey here"—I pointed to her—"is a reporter for *Rolling Stone* magazine."

"Oh, so it's a show and tell?" There was sarcasm in her tone, but she was smiling.

Casey didn't miss a beat. She leaned in and asked, "What did you bring to show and tell, Hazel?"

"I got stories, kid. But we're old school around here. If it ain't mine to tell, I'm not telling."

"Well, what *can* you tell me, Hazel?" Casey smiled, leaning back on her stool.

Hazel took a deep breath. "She was a good kid, talented. We all knew that she was something special right from the start. I was standing right here with her mom the first time we heard her song on the radio. Kat's momma worked here too. The restaurant was full. It was lunchtime and everyone put their forks down. Everyone in town is a Kat Bennett fan and has been since she was a girl, so hearing her voice come through the radio just about knocked our socks off. When the song was through, the whole place broke into applause and people started hugging and kissing Kat's momma. Her name's Miriam, by the way, Kat's momma."

I blushed, I'd heard that story before but it made me feel happy. I turned to Casey.

"My mom and Hazel are friends."

"And now your mom lives in New York with you?" We'd covered this ground earlier, but it was a conversation I didn't mind having so we could hang out here all day. "Yes. As soon as I could, I brought her to me. We're close, and I like having her nearby. Every now and then, she comes back here to visit. With touring and recording, it was just too hard to..."

I was interrupted by the jingling bell on the cafe door. A hulk of a man walked in, hollering, "Heeeeeyzeeeel!" He was almost singing the word. "We need pie. What do you have in store for us today, you sweet ray of sunshine?"

When he caught sight of me, the hunky cowboy dead stopped with a stunned look on his face. It took me a second. When I left Conway, this hulk of a man was a pimply-faced fourteen-year-old kid. This was Wyatt Morgan. One of Billy's little brothers.

Behind Wyatt, another man came in; he must have been looking down at his phone. All I could see was the tipping brim of his hat. He said, "She's asking for cherry," right before he ran smack-dab into Wyatt's back. "What the heck, Wyatt?"

He couldn't see me, and I couldn't see him. But I knew his voice better than my own: Billy Morgan.

3

BILLY

I was utterly silent. Shell-shocked. Standing there like a mute idiot. For the last ten years, I'd lain awake in bed at night thinking of all the things I'd say to Kat Bennett if I ever saw her, and now she was standing in front of me and I couldn't even make my tongue say, *Hey*.

It was like my mouth was full of cotton balls, all fuzzy and dry. I should have been yelling or kissing or apologizing. Something. At the very least talking about the weather. But nada. I was just staring, like a creepy-ass mofo. I couldn't stop staring. Looking at her, my whole body screamed yes. That girl right there is yours. Go to her. Take her. She has always been yours. She will always be yours. But my mind knew better. Even if I still wanted her, she wasn't mine. A long time ago I was young, broken, and stupid and I watched her walk away. What we had couldn't be revived.

While my mouth was paralyzed, my dick was not. One glance had me all riled up in an instant. I knew she wasn't mine to want anymore, but in some ways, she still looked like the girl I loved all those years ago—auburn hair cascading down her back, inquisitive hazel eyes, long lean curves for days. Sure, her jeans were ripped without any other wear, and for some unknown reason, the bottoms of her shoes were painted red, but she was still damn sexy. And her eyes still revved my engine.

She was watching me. Of course, she was still making words. She was poised, elegant. Like only a public figure could, she held it together, laughing and talking like nothing even vaguely amiss was taking place. But I could feel her watching me. Her eyes would drift in my direction, and I could see the clouds there. There was a time when I knew Kat better than I knew myself, and if I didn't know better, I would tell you she was hurting.

That was the thing about Kat, what we had wasn't only about getting hard and getting off. We were best friends. We caught frogs together. We shared cotton candy at the county fair. When I was twelve, I carried her from the creek to my house when she sprained her ankle. I could sit for hours with her in her room listening to her music, cracking jokes and shooting the shit long before she let me kiss her.

The first time I kissed her, she was sitting on the same stool she was sitting on now. I was sixteen and Kat was almost sixteen. I'd known she was more than my best friend since we'd gone through puberty, but crossing a friendship line that deep took a certain kind of bravery. It was a school night. Kat was closing for Hazel. She closed up for Hazel a lot. I hated the idea of her riding her bike home late at night. So, as soon as I got my license, I started picking her up and driving her home. I liked the closeness of having her in the cab of my truck, the heat of her thigh just inches from mine, the aching need to reach my hand out and caress her flesh.

When I got to the cafe that night, Kat hadn't quite finished her work, so she unlocked the door and let me in. The music was on and she was mopping. She warmed up a slice of pie for me and it was sitting on the counter. I took a seat and ate, watching her mop. She danced and sang as she worked, and the gyrations of her hips had me pressing against the zipper in my jeans. There wasn't a day that went by when I wasn't wishing I could pull those hips to me and press her hard against my need. Back then I wasn't experienced enough to know what I wanted to do to Kat, but I considered it. I imagined her every which way, beneath me, on top of me, on her knees in front of me, bent over that counter with my cock buried deep inside her. However, until that night, anything even vaguely sexual between us was just in my fantasies.

When she finished mopping, Kat ditched the bucket in the kitchen and came to sit on the stool next to me. We were facing each other, and I couldn't tell you for certain why that was the moment. I don't know if it was because she was so beautiful, her hair all mussed and her skin flushed from hard work, or if I was just so damn in love with her that it burst out of me, but I looked at her and said, "Kat, I'm gonna kiss you now."

She smiled, a 'light up yer whole damn face' smile. And then my mouth was on hers. I was nervous for like a split second. I worried that I didn't know what I was doing, but her lips parted, and it was like a dam broke. She was soft and wet, and I wanted to devour her. Kat was giving as good as she got. I almost felt like she was trying to climb into my lap, pushing her whole body at me, but being trapped by the space between the two stools.

So, I did what any sex-crazed hormonal teenager with ranch-trained biceps would do. I picked her up and tossed her on the counter in front of me. We broke apart when I moved her, and Kat giggled. When I looked into her eyes, she bit her lower lip.

"This okay?" I asked, knowing full well that it was.

She nodded.

I bowed my head and kissed her neck, the spot between her jawline and her ear. It was a flutter of a kiss, a simple graze of my lips, but Kat dropped her head back and let out a slow moan. I'd never heard her make that sound before, but I immediately wanted to hear it again. I swept my fingertips up from her waist, slowly. I wanted to feel the weight of her breasts in my hands, but I wasn't sure she'd let me. Kat didn't rebuke me. Instead, she took my hand in hers and moved it so that I was cradling her breast. Kat's tits were better than I imagined. Beneath the fabric of her uniform, they were plush and firm at the same time, and I could feel the hard little peak of her nipple, begging for my caress. I gently pinched the tight little nub and there was that sound again.

Instinctually, I pulled her hips flush against my hard length like I'd imagined doing twenty minutes before. And then she was saying words, breathy, disconnected words.

"Oh God, Billy... Billy, is that your... Holy shit. It's so big."

Talk about a good night.

I had loved Kat Bennett as a friend and a partner. We were in diapers together. Kat stood next to me in every Halloween, Thanksgiving, and Christmas photo for the first nineteen years of my life. I thought we were forever. I thought I knew her. But it was a long time ago. The girl giggling and moaning as I kissed her on that stool didn't leave me behind. This Kat, the one in front of me sitting tall, tight, and elegant, chose fame and fortune over me and never looked back. She didn't care that my mom died a couple of years before she left me or that my brothers were too young to really help my dad. She didn't give a shit about my responsibilities.

So, to hell with sweet sixteen-year-old Kat who got me all riled up. The only Kat in the room was the famous one, and I'd never met her before. Honestly, I didn't care to.

If Wyatt would've just shut up, we could've grabbed our cherry pie and left by now. He'd already told three embarrassing stories about Kat. I was thankful he was keeping my name out of the muck. But, honestly, I didn't have faith that his discretion would hold out.

The guy who Kat introduced as Marcus took a step back to take a phone call, and I used that moment to elbow Wyatt, a not so subtle signal that it was time for us to go. Wyatt made no move to say anything, so I took it upon myself to get the show on the road. "Hazel, if it wouldn't be too much trouble, can we get that cherry pie? Gotta be home by six for dinner."

Hazel pursed her lips at me, obviously not feeling my failure to talk to Kat, but still she obliged my request. I turned my attention to the circle of people Wyatt was talking to, tipped my hat, and said, "Lovely meeting y'all."

Wyatt seemed to take my lead, saying, "Well, guess we gotta go. My brother, Captain Organization, calls. It was good seeing ya, Kat. Welcome 'round anytime." He took the pie from Hazel, and I turned toward the door. I could feel Wyatt step behind me, but then he stopped. "Ya know, Casey, I bet you'd get a kick out of seeing Kat's old house."

"Yes, I so would."

Instantly, I hated Wyatt. He was a no good, very bad, terrible brother.

I was pretty sure Kat hated him too. She narrowed her eyes in his direction. She didn't want that reporter in our house any more than I did. Kat had shattered me. Hurt me almost irreparably, but she never prostituted what we had, even though her first album was all about us. She never told a single reporter about our love, never. In a sort of sweet way, I was her dirty little secret.

Kat's shoulders were tight and even if no one else could tell, I knew the saccharine tone in her voice when she said, "That's awfully sweet of you, Wyatt. We would, but we're on a schedule and I've got to get back to New York tonight."

Perfect cover, Kat. Take that, Wyatt, you meddling idiot.

And then, that Marcus guy reappeared. He seemed almost skittish when he said, "Actually, it looks like that flight out tonight is going to be delayed."

4

KAT

In the car, it really hit me. I saw Billy Morgan, my Billy. The boy who wrecked me for all others, and much to my chagrin, he looked good. He was bigger. He was a muscular guy at nineteen. I remembered hours running my hand over the ripples of his abs as a teenager, but the man version of Billy was more than rippling abs. He was big, broad shoulders, and arms so bulky that the fabric of his shirt pulled tight across his biceps. The softness of boyhood had left his face. His jaw was angular and shadowed with scruff. The eyes were the same though—the bright blue of the sky on a clear sun-shined day, my blue-eyed beau.

There were other things about him that felt different. When Billy looked at me ten years ago, he was light. He was solid but also mischievous. When you were in the room with him, it was fun. He was always ready to play. Grown-up Billy didn't radiate that anymore. He was on task and the light that made everyone want to know him and be friends with him ... that light was gone. I wanted to feel angry, but seeing him made me feel everything but anger.

I felt sick about it, my stomach writhing. I was nervous. He made me nervous, made my tongue thick in my mouth. I was sad that he didn't look happy. I was desperate. I wanted to corner him, tell him again that I wasn't making a choice. I was loving him and music at the same time. We had been so young. I had a dream. It was offered to me, but it didn't have to mean that I didn't want him too. I also ached to touch him. I was physically drawn to him, pulled to him like a magnet. All those years ago, he'd given me an ultimatum—him or New York. I said no. I said don't make me choose and wondered why I couldn't have both. I was already in New York when he decided it was one or the other, and with the wheels in motion, I couldn't drop everything and run back. And then he stopped taking my calls.

I got angry because I needed to stop being sad. I decided I never wanted to return to Conway or be near him again. I realized that the love of men was unreliable. So, I brought my mom to New York and sold her house because the thought of Billy haunted me. And now, a few minutes of watching him glower at me in Hazel's and I was tied up in knots after working ten years to try to unfurl them. Forget what I said, I felt angry.

The drive to my old house was about ten minutes. We followed Billy's' big ol' dark-blue truck down the dirt road. I was surprised he had the same truck. Who keeps a truck for over ten years? When we got to my old house, Wyatt jumped out and Billy drove on to his folks' place, dust billowing behind the tires as he peeled off. I felt relieved that he was gone. I found myself smiling quietly, imagining the earful Wyatt was subject to on that drive.

When we got out of the car and stood in front of the house, the same thing that happened when Hazel hugged me happened again. The house was a Victorian-style beauty with a wraparound porch. Standing there looking at the well-cared-for and recently painted decorative trim, I had this teary-eyed hollow in the pit of my stomach. It was like I had a locked treasure box inside me, and these people and these things were prying it open. And the thing was, inside this treasure box, there weren't gold coins and gems; instead, there was this hot white light that was burning through the thick skin I had worked so hard to develop. As a celebrity, a thick skin was my shield against everything—bad reviews, tabloid nonsense, failed relationships, no privacy, all the things that made being famous a nightmare. The girl who lived in this house didn't have to be afraid of people who looked and acted like friends but weren't. I felt loved in this town, and I loved the people in it. Until Billy ended our relationship, and then there was nothing here for me.

Everything about the house was shocking. First, as he was unlocking the door, Wyatt explained that he and Billy lived in the house. Billy lived in my house? Was that an effing joke? And then once I was inside, it was like a time warp. I mean, I knew they didn't tear down the house, but I wasn't expecting it to be exactly as I left it, same furniture, same everything. I mean, my gram's tea towel was hanging over the oven handle.

Okay, it was sort of different. It was covered in man. I mean, what is it about guys that just changes the aura of a place? It felt weird that Billy lived in my house. It felt weird that any dudes lived in my house. There were never guys in our house. It was me and my momma and my gram, who died when I was ten. It was a house filled with women and women things and now it was packed with big menfolk. Wyatt and Billy were raised right, so it's not like the place was dirty. It just somehow smelled different. And there were hats and boots strewn about. Actually, it was kinda manic, about half of the hats and boots were lined up in tidy lines. Billy and Wyatt were always of different dispositions, so I was guessing that their different personalities accounted for the varying degrees of mess. Again, it's not like it was a hovel. Just the feeling of dudes everywhere.

So yeah, the house made me feel weird, and I was having a hard time managing that feeling and Casey's questions. But that didn't stop her from asking them. So far, she had gleaned that the Morgans were family to me, which was something I'd kept pretty quiet up until now because I didn't want the press to bother them. It just sort of slipped out that with our house and their house being so close, we were connected. Also, Duke Morgan, Billy's father, was an old school patriarch, and it just didn't sit well with him, three women living alone with no man about the house. He looked after us, even though we were perfectly capable of looking after ourselves.

Casey had also gleaned that the house was all but untouched. I felt like she was nudging around that, trying to figure out why anyone would move into someone else's house and not alter a thing. But since I didn't really know, she wasn't getting anything out of me. So, she asked Wyatt, "Didn't you or your brother want to make this place your own?"

Up until this point, Wyatt had proved himself quite the troublemaker, but he played off her question like only a ranch boy could. "Why? Everything in here works perfectly well.

No need to change things. If it ain't broke, don't fix it, amiright?"

Casey smiled but was clearly not satisfied with his answer. "Can I take some pictures?" she asked.

I didn't really want her to, but Wyatt shrugged his approval, and honestly, that's why I was on this PR disaster tour, right? Casey proceeded to poke around the bottom floor and June followed her because June was good like that. She always had my back. Wyatt stayed back in the kitchen with me.

"I think it's best we don't go upstairs," he said under his breath conspiratorially to me. I looked at him, my eyes wide. What would she find upstairs? "It's gonna be harder to explain why your old room is frozen in time, don't ya think?"

My room was the same too? I had an instinct to turn and head straight up the stairs, but I didn't. Wait, why wasn't one of them using my room? My room got the best light and had the most windows.

Wyatt read the curiosity on my face. "He won't change it, Kat. If you ask me, it's not so complicated."

I needed a drink. I crossed the room and opened the fridge, which was also strange. Hanging at the top of the left side was a label that read "Bill" and on the right was a label that said "Wyatt." Bill's side was a series of well-organized labeled items; they were marked with the date, and some even looked like meal prep, marked with the weekday and the mealtime. Was Billy really a sergeant in the cold storage commandos? Wyatt's side featured a bottle of ketchup, a funky-looking apple, and a half-empty six-pack of beer in cans. I looked to Wyatt for an explanation. He rolled his eyes but didn't get to respond because the back door, which led right into the kitchen, slammed open and Sarah Morgan, the only girl child in the Morgan clan, clamored through in a huff. "Honestly," she whined. "You're in Conway and you didn't tell me?"

Sarah and I had secretly exchanged emails for the last ten years. When Billy and I broke up, I couldn't just leave her all alone in a house full of guys—and the Morgan men were like guys with a capital G. Her mother died when she was eight and even if I wasn't with Billy, she still needed a woman in her life. I mean, I was the one who helped her through her first period. Plus, I loved her. I also wrote Duke a few letters a year. He was as close as I ever got to having a father. I couldn't just walk away. The boys had Billy. But I needed Duke and Sarah, and they needed me. In our exchanges, neither one of them ever mentioned Billy and I never asked. It was like the unwritten rule of our continued communication.

I didn't know what to say about not telling her I was coming to Conway. I'd hoped I'd get in and out without anyone knowing, but now that she was standing in front of me, I knew that it was terrible that I didn't tell her.

"I should have," I said. I took a step toward her. "That wasn't right. I'm sorry." Even though we stayed in touch, I hadn't seen her in years. I mean, a photo here and there, but standing across from her was so different. She wasn't a little girl anymore. She was a woman, a tall, pretty brunette who looked a lot like Molly, her late mom. "God, Sarah," I smiled. "You're so beautiful."

"Shut up," she pout-smiled. "I'm trying hard to be mad at you."

I hugged her and after a beat, she lifted her arms and hugged me in return.

When we broke apart, Wyatt said, "You didn't make a move to hug me like that ... I see how it is."

I sucker punched him in the arm.

"You had a 'no girls allowed' sign on your bedroom door," Sarah retorted. "Why would she still be friends with you?"

"I missed all of you," I said, smiling, happy to be back in the middle of their banter, and then immediately blushed, realizing how my words could be misinterpreted.

At that moment, Casey and June walked back into the kitchen, and Marcus, who had been out in the SUV making phone calls to try to manage our flight, came in behind them. I immediately looked to Marcus, hoping for some good news.

He shook his head. That wasn't good.

"What's the word?" I asked.

"Grounded tonight and maybe tomorrow, snow and ice. We're just not getting out of here all that soon, Kat."

I sucked in a deep breath. Trapped in Conway. This was literally my nightmare.

Beside me, Sarah started to jump up and down, excited. "Oh yay! That's so good." Then she took in the tone of the room and asked, "Isn't it?"

Marcus continued, "It gets worse. Not enough room at the inn."

"The Dew Drop?" Wyatt asked.

Marcus nodded and then said, "Only three rooms."

I sighed. "Listen, that's okay. June and I will camp out together. It's fine."

"Don't be ridiculous," Sarah said. "You'll stay here. This is your house. Plus, you have to see Daddy. Ohhhh, and I'm singing at Sadie's on Sunday. You should come. Oh my God, will you come?" She was talking so fast.

"Umm..." I didn't see an easy way out of this situation.

Wyatt smirked, "Ab-so-lute-ly. You should so stay here, Kat. That is a fantastic idea."

5

BILLY

I was sulking on the couch in my father's living room. I was acting like a giant baby. The way I saw it, Wyatt should have felt happy that I wasn't keying his truck. What kind of a man invites his older brother's ex-soulmate back to their house? A jerk, that's who. Sometimes a man just has to be sour and the people around him can suck it up. My father came into the room carrying an iced tea and sat down in his recliner. My father wasn't a big talker. He was the stoic kind that skulked in the corner and only talked when he deemed it absolutely necessary.

So, I was surprised when he said, "I heard your Kit-Kat is back."

I scoffed, "My Kit-Kat. Come on, Dad." Still sulking.

"Make no mistake, Bill, that girl's your girl. Apart or together, you belong to her."

The stoic old codger was a die-hard romantic. My father loved Kat. He always had. I stood up. It was so irritating. "Just stop it with that nonsense. It's been ten years. It's not

like we had a fight, Dad. Kat Bennett is a stranger that we all
once knew."

I stomped off, but before I crossed out of the room, he grumbled, "Stubborn mule."

I couldn't go to my house—which always felt a little like
Kat's house—because now it would definitely feel like Kat's
house because Kat was in it. Trapped, I just lingered in my
father's kitchen, poured myself a glass of iced tea, and
waited for the coast to clear.

I couldn't break free of the film reel of Kat in my head. Kat
laughing at me from across the dinner table. Kat with her
face pressed into my shoulder at a horror movie. Kat's hair
spread out across my lap at dusk, near a bonfire. Kat
brushing my little sister's hair. Kat looking at me with utter
affection because I freed a kitten from chicken wire. Kat
crying at my momma's funeral. Kat on the stool at Hazel's as
beautiful as ever.

I thought I'd feel relief when I heard the gravel sputter
under Kat's SUV, a rock-solid good-riddance-to-my-old-
baggage feeling. Only, it didn't feel that way at all. Instead, I
felt a cool emptiness in my chest. I had a chance to say
something. I had a chance to take on the mess that I'd been
carrying on my shoulders for ten years, and I literally said
nothing at all. I don't know what I could have said. But the
idea that she was gone again curdled my stomach. The girl
who wasn't my girl was gone again.

I needed to clear my head, so I decided to go back to the
house and shower before dinner. I hollered to my father,
"I'm gonna clean up before we eat." And then I headed
toward the front door. As I pivoted to reach for the knob, I

looked through the windowpane and saw Kat and Sarah coming toward the house. They were smiling. Sarah looked happy. It was a different happy than I'd seen in a long time. Sarah wasn't a glass half empty kind of girl, so she looked happy a lot, but what was passing between her and Kat was something special. They were laughing in the way girls laugh together. Sarah didn't have a lot of that. For a second, I was glad that they were together. And then feeling good while looking at Kat scrambled my brain, so I turned, headed upstairs, and hid in my littlest brother's bedroom to collect myself.

I paced back and forth in Cody's room. Cody was Sarah's twin. His room smelled like sweat socks. I told myself, *I'm a man, not a sixteen-year-old boy. I basically run a ranch. I am the oldest of four brothers and one bossy little sister. I am not about to let some old flame make me weak in the knees.* I needed a new plan. Avoiding Kat wasn't an option. Maybe it was time to bury the hatchet. Was I capable of that? It had been ten years. My father cared about Kat, Sarah cared about Kat, and I was keeping her from them. Maybe I could try to be the bigger man. A part of me was afraid that letting Kat in a little wasn't an option for me, that it was an all or nothing situation. But maybe a friendship with Kat would be good. Maybe if I let her in a little, having her near me would mean I wouldn't have to feel so sad that I lost her in the first place.

Downstairs, I heard male voices, which meant that Cody and Wyatt had arrived. The house started to smell like food. And I knew if I didn't go down soon, everyone would already be sitting at the table by the time I entered the room. I didn't want that. I wanted to go into the dining room with everyone else. I headed to the kitchen because I was pretty sure that everyone but my dad would be in there.

They always were. Somehow, even at a party, my family was always gathered in the kitchen.

I smiled as I walked in, let my eyes drift to Cody, and nodded my head in hello. There was a lot of silence. Everyone was staring at me. I crossed to the refrigerator and said, "I'm gonna have a beer. Anyone want one? Kat?" I leaned into the fridge, took a beer, and then glanced over my shoulder for confirmation. My siblings weren't looking at me anymore; instead, they were looking at Kat.

"I could have a beer," she said. Her tone was soft, sweet. And just like that, the ice in my chest started to melt.

6

KAT

Part of me felt like I had crossed over into the Twilight Zone. I was standing in the Morgans' dining room trying to decide where to sit. Growing up, I sat next to Billy. And considering he just spoke to me and handed me a beer, I didn't want to offend by not sitting next to him, but then again, I wasn't sure I could handle being that close to him all through dinner. Also, was it weird that a part of me wondered if he poisoned my beer? I mean, a few hours ago, the guy didn't even acknowledge I was in the room and now he was gifting me things? Seemed suspect, don't ya think? So yeah, I just stood there, stymied.

Duke saved me from my own tribulations. "Kit-Kat, come sit next to me."

No one had called me Kit-Kat in a long time. I was always Kit-Kat in this house and being her again felt like Goldilocks in baby bear's chair—just right. I followed Duke's lead and sat to his left. Sarah was on his right. Wyatt next to me and Cody next to her. Billy sat at the opposite end of the table across from Duke. When I was a kid, we needed the leaf in the dining table, but with Molly gone and my family in New York, the table was smaller. If Luke, the second oldest Morgan boy, had been there, we would have had to add a chair.

"Where's Luke?" I asked. Luke was by far the brother I was closest to besides Billy. We had kept in touch for a while after I left but talking to him reminded me too much of Billy, so we agreed to talk less and eventually not at all.

Sarah answered. "Got an apartment in town. Doesn't come for dinner most of the time because he's engaged now." She passed a platter of mashed potatoes as she spoke. "Her name is Maddie. We hardly recognize him. He's so happy all the time."

"Was he not happy?" I asked.

"Noooooo... apparently, we were too hard on the big softy," Wyatt ribbed. "Well, there was never any comparison to ol' giggly Bill over here." He swung his thumbs at Billy. "But Luke was feeling kinda closeted by our roasting of his artistic talents. He's an artist, ya know?"

"He was always an artist," I said. "Remember when we missed our school photos? Luke drew our class pictures, and they were so good that they printed them in the yearbook."

Duke smiled.

Cody snickered, then added, "Luke's fine. He's head over heels. These fools are just too much up in everyone's business."

"I'd love to see him," I offered.

"Well, maybe if we knew you were coming," Sarah needled.

Duke squelched the banter. "Okay, enough sibling smack talk. We haven't seen this beauty in a while, and I don't know if you all realized, but girl done good. Tell us about being a big-time rock 'n' roller, Kat. Your tour's going to Australia this spring, right?"

I knew right away that Duke's knowledge of my upcoming tour was going to trip alarms for the boys, but for a split second, I hoped it might go unnoticed. It didn't.

Wyatt guffawed, "Dad, are you following Kat on the internet?"

Duke looked a little flustered for a second. And then the man in him got centered. He looked down at his plate and worked at cutting his chicken when he said, "I'll let you worry about the internet, Wyatt. Kit-Kat here keeps me up to date about her life in good ol'-fashioned letters, with hand-written addresses and stamps, thank you very much."

Everyone got real quiet. Billy stopped chewing. He looked at me. "You write Dad letters?"

I nodded.

"For how long?" He didn't think he looked angry. I couldn't tell. Was he angry?

I took a deep breath. I was an international superstar. I could answer this question. "About ten years. Give or take a few months."

"Why?" Billy asked.

I didn't hesitate. "Because they're my family too."

Billy looked around the room, not angry but maybe a little accusatory. "All of you?"

The Morgan boys were in the clear and it showed on their faces. Sarah, on the other hand, made a goofy face and then literally started to sink under the table. And by literally, I mean *literally*. She hid under the table.

Billy laughed, and then we were all laughing.

Billy broke into the cacophony of giggles, asking, "Hey, y'all remember the time Kat baked Dad a birthday cake?"

Sarah and Cody were too young to remember.

Billy continued. "She baked it in the morning. Worked so hard on it, even wrote 'Happy Birthday Duke' out in icing, and then she put the cake in the cupboard so Dad wouldn't see it. She wanted to surprise him."

Sarah, someone who actually cooked, said, "Dad's birthday is in August."

"Sure is," Billy said.

Duke started chuckling.

I finished the story for him. "It was cake soup."

Duke added his two cents. "Still delicious."

I laughed. "That is absolutely not true. It was terrible. And if I remember correctly, Wyatt put his plate on the floor and Cody, you got on all fours and pretended it was dog food."

Duke tried to control himself, holding his breath, and then he laughed again. "It was terrible."

Billy smiled. "Thought that counts, right, Pop?"

Duke smiled at me again and shook his head. "You were so disappointed. And it was so sweet."

"You know what wasn't sweet?" I asked rhetorically. "The time Wyatt put Nair in Billy and Luke's shampoo."

Wyatt laughed. "That's so basic, who still falls for that?"

"Billy and Luke." I laughed with him.

Billy quipped, "I'll have you know, I looked very sexy with no hair."

"You did." It just sort of popped out.

There was a beat, and then Wyatt said, "Luke didn't."

And we were all laughing again.

The stories continued. The time Sarah painted the front door pink for breast cancer awareness because the school said students needed to think of a way to support women and she took that very seriously. The time Cody hid what he thought was a little mouse in his bedroom; only, it turned out that mouse was a legit rat. The time Billy ripped his shorts at the lake and had an impromptu and very public skinny-dipping experience. I laughed so hard my belly ached.

"We have to stop," I said, trying to catch my breath.

Sarah started to gather the dishes and Wyatt stood up too. "Well," he said. "Before I get roped into cleaning up. I got a date."

"A date?" Billy asked skeptically.

"When do you have a date?" Cody echoed.

"When I do. I have dates," Wyatt said like they were both ridiculous.

"Yeah, and I have wings," Cody said.

"You have bar hookups," Billy chided.

"Well, tonight, I got a date." Wyatt leaned over and kissed the side of my head. "See you in the morning, Kit-Kat."

And then he was gone, and Billy and I were still with everyone—but also very much alone for the evening.

After learning that Kat had stayed in contact with my dad and Sarah for all those years, I felt drawn to her, protective even. It touched me that she cared about them, that she worried about them and still wanted to know about their lives. Her love for them felt big, like even though I felt deserted by her for a decade, she was still out there wondering and worrying about things that were important to me. She didn't leave us all behind, just me. And I was mature enough now to see that it was complicated but back then I felt lost. I could see her leaving and I couldn't stop her. I didn't know how to explain to her that I knew there were no choices. She couldn't have her music and have me, so maybe I chose for her because I couldn't bear not being chosen. Maybe we deserted each other. Maybe all this time I just needed someone else to blame.

The snow was coming down hard, and there was no way that I was gonna let Kat walk back, no matter how awkward it would feel to sit in the cab of my truck together. The gentleman in me just couldn't fathom it. So, rather than cutting out like Wyatt, I rolled up my sleeves and got down and dirty in a whole lot of soapy dishes. Kat and Sarah dried. When the dishes were done, there was no room for excuses. It was time for us to go back to Kat's old house, my current one.

While we put on our coats, Sarah stood at the door with us. She was bouncing from one foot to the other. She emanated this weird restrained energy that might just pop like a soda can that you dropped before opening. I put my hand on her shoulder to quiet her movement and said, "You got something you need to say, kiddo?" Sarah was always my baby sister, no matter how old she got—always a kid to me.

"It's just... it's really nice to have you two be nice to each other. Try not to screw it up, okay?" This wasn't directed specifically at me. She was talking to Kat too.

Kat hugged her. Then held her shoulders at arm's length, looking Sarah right in the eyes. "We will do our best." Kat looked at me. "Right?"

I nodded and winked at my kid sister. Then I pulled the door with my left hand and held it open near the top, allowing Kat to duck under my arm and head out onto the porch. As she grazed by me, I caught a whiff of her shampoo. Same scent as always. I was transported into the past, a flash of my hand in her hair, pulling her head back to kiss her neck. She was naked on my lap, her skin sweaty and plush in my hands as she slowly rode my cock. The memory stirred up a current physical response, and I was suddenly pretty damn hard beneath my jeans. Whoops. I tried to subtly adjust myself. Then, as I closed the door, I gave my bigger head a good shake, trying to unring that particular bell.

Kat had already started to head down the porch steps. Those silly shoes of hers were absolutely useless. She was gripping the banister as if it were a lifeline, rightfully so. A snowstorm like this would create icy surfaces. Even still, she looked hot from behind. Her jacket stopped just above the curve of her ass. I imagined that she had personal trainers and chefs on her payroll, but I swear to God that was the same sweet fleshy bottom I chased as a teenager.

I followed her down the steps. She got to the yard just fine and then turned around and did a little celebratory dance. It was the jig that got her. That and those stupid red-bottomed heels. Since I often took the steps three at a time, I was able to catch her. My only choice was to crush her to my chest before she hit the ground. Kat in my arms minutes after I remembered her naked and ogled her ass was complicated.

I had her lifted off the ground, her lips inches from mine. I could feel her breasts pressed against my chest. I didn't know if it was because I was holding her or because she nearly fell, but her breath was coming out fast and hard.

My heart pounded, and as expected, there was less blood in my brain than usual. When I spoke, my voice came out deep and rough with need. "You okay, Kat?"

She bit her lip. I would have bet the ranch she was wet. She swallowed and took a deep breath, her chest heaving. Even though I couldn't feel them through her coat, I knew she was pushing her nipples tighter against my pecs. One more deep breath to regain composure and then she nodded, signaling that she was okay, and I could put her down.

I set her on the ground gently but kept my hand on her arm, leading her to the truck. I pulled the door open and lifted her up into my cab by wrapping my hands around her hips, and then I settled her into the seat. Like a homing pigeon on autopilot, I buckled her seat belt, something I used to do a long time ago. Something I'd never done for anyone else. I used to kiss her too, sometimes get carried away enough to unbuckle the seat belt I'd just buckled. Thankfully, I was in control enough not to do that. Instead, I shut the passenger door and trudged over to the driver's side of the truck.

The drive was only a couple of minutes, and we were both quiet. As teenagers whenever she was in my truck, I'd rest my hand on her thigh, and I was aching to do that, even though I had no right to. I stopped the car in the driveway to the house. Kat looked out the windshield at her old home. Her granddaddy built it. It was part of her history, which was why I couldn't bring myself to change it.

"She's still a pretty old girl," she said wistfully.

"Sure is," I said.

She gave me a flirty look. "Don't talk about me like that, Billy Morgan. I'm not old yet."

I smiled at her stupid joke.

She looked back out the window. "Thank you for tonight. I missed them all so much." She was sad. Her loneliness was billowing around us like a cloud. "I don't laugh like that anymore."

"It was fun," I said lamely, not knowing how to tell her that I loved it too. I huffed out a breath, and nodding to the passenger side, said, "I'll come around." I popped open my door and jumped out. The air was cold on my cheeks.

She undid her seat belt before I got there, and instead of lifting her out, I just supported her when she climbed down on her own. I held the crook of her elbow as we headed to the house and climbed the steps to the door. I felt weird pulling my key from my pocket, like I'd locked her out of her house. Once inside Kat hung her jacket on the coatrack and then stood uncomfortably in the hallway.

"Can I get you anything?" I asked.

"I'm good," she said. "I think I'll just head up to bed."

"You know the way. Bed's clean," I offered.

"Really? The bed's clean?"

"We have a woman who cleans, Kat. It's not a museum. It's a guest room." *That no one had ever stayed in.*

"Of course," she confirmed. She headed toward the stairs, and I got to look at her ass one more time before she turned and said, "Night, Billy."

Kat was the only one who ever called me Billy.

Wyatt was not kidding. Billy might be calling my room a guest room, but only if his guests were really into bands from 2003 and a lot of photos of my high school friends. Also, how often was this woman washing my sheets because the pale purple ones I lost my virginity on were still not threadbare. I pulled open the closet door. Dresses, shoes, all the things I didn't take to New York ten years ago. I crossed to the dresser, pulled open the second drawer, pajamas. That was convenient. Although, I never imagined that I'd be wearing a floor-length flannel nightgown again.

What did it mean? Why did he keep my room like this for all these years? It was a little bit like taxidermy, and by that, I mean like a creepy shrine to a me that was long ago forgotten, like a teenage version of me was stuffed and mounted in the basement. Only, it was also sad and sort of sweet. I mean, I didn't feel like Billy was sitting around for the last ten years pining for me. In fact, I felt like he spent the last ten years hating me because I chose to follow my dream of being a musician. But maybe I was wrong. Maybe it wasn't about pining for me or hating me (or preserving me). Maybe it was about saving the memory of what we had before it blew up. Billy was part of me. He was part of my foundation. My time with him influenced every relationship I'd ever had. Whether I realized it or not, I compared them all to him. And I don't just mean emotionally.

How sad was it that the sexiest man I'd ever known was the first man I slept with? Maybe it was because we knew everything about each other, but having sex with Billy was earth-shattering, every time. Maybe it was just chemistry. I mean, when he caught me and kept me from falling earlier, it took every ounce of control in my body not to straight-up moan his name. His hands weren't even on my skin. We were just close, but being close to Billy was enough to make me start shivering. And it was the same for him, I know it. I heard it in his voice.

Billy was my kryptonite. Too much time around him and I was a goner. I had to get out of Conway before I lost sight of what was important. But for the time being, I was stuck, so there was no real harm in strolling down memory lane. If he wanted to be friendly, I could do that. We had a good night. And really, I loved the Morgan family, so peace with Billy was in my best interest. I just had to keep a little physical distance between us.

I pulled my old granny gown over my head and laughed at myself in the mirror. If I could just wear a flannel monstrosity all the time, the chemistry might fizzle. I kept my socks on, knowing in my bones that my room was always drafty. As I pulled the covers back and curled up in my old bed, I thought, *man, it's good to be home*. And then I was sleeping.

I FELT the warmth of his soft lips on my left ankle, the strength of his hand gripping my right. He fluttered kisses up my calf, swirled his tongue behind my knee, etched a path of kneading hands and mouth across my thighs. Billy, under the covers. I was still groggy with sleep, but the feeling was delicious and familiar.

He never dove right in. Instead, he lingered, hot breath inches from my core. Ran his fingertips back and forth over the crease where my leg turned into my center. A tantalizing kiss here or there, the wetness of his mouth promising pleasure, but not quite yet.

I arched my hips toward him, keeping my eyes closed. "Please..."

He offered me only one finger. slowly dragging it from the top of my clit, down the peak, and up again. And again. So slow. And the lightest touch. A torture.

"Please..." I begged again.

Two fingers now. Inside me. I pushed against his hand, desperate and wet. Fucking his fingers but wanting so much more. He always waited until I was on the edge.

And then his mouth, hot and slippery between my thighs. Fuck, finally. I pushed my hands through his thick brown hair. He had taken off his shirt, but he was still wearing jeans and my feet clawed against the denim. I was absolutely reckless with desire. Wanton and bucking, coiling toward my release.

At first, a little spark, an ember glowing and growing from my sex, catching like wildfire, lighting up every nerve. Then a blaze, an uncontrollable combustion of contracting muscles and guttural cries, the near-blindness of passion.

And then the sewing needle shaking of spent legs, the brush of his chest against mine as he climbed toward my mouth, the cool hardness of his belt buckle on my tender, shivering folds, the press of his own desperation, still caged in his jeans pushing against my thigh, the flavor of my pussy on his lips. The morning sun filtering through the blinds, and the alarm.

My cell phone alarm?

MY CELL PHONE ALARM. I opened my eyes. It was morning and I was still in my teenage bedroom. Sadly, or maybe thankfully, Billy was not there. Oh, yeah, I needed to get out of Conway. Figuring it was best to get up and get going before I ran into Billy, I dug around in my closet and drawers, unearthing some old jeans and a comfy blue sweater. I also found a pair of old boots.

I tiptoed down the hall, boots in hand, being careful not to make a sound. Each creak of the floor had my nerves on edge. Once I was in the kitchen, I sat down at the table, pulled on my boots, and texted June. I chose June over Marcus because she wouldn't give me an entire itinerary unless I asked. Marcus was a great manager, but he liked to hear himself talk and text.

Me: *Any news?*

June: *Not today, Jose.*

Me: *You guys okay?*

The little pulsing ellipsis signaling that she was writing pulsed for longer than I would have thought.

June: *Yep.*

Not what I expected based on wait time, but okay.

Me: *Keep me posted.*

June: *That's the job :P*

Okay, so if I was spending another day down home with the Morgans, then it was going to be with Sarah. I grabbed my jacket and headed out the door. For sure, Sarah would be up soon. Ranchers liked breakfast and coffee early.

It was still cold out, but the snow had stopped. I'd been living in the city for a long time. I couldn't remember the last time I crunched snow under my boots. I felt like a kid again. I could see the barn in the distance. To the average onlooker, it was just a big old red barn with an older style hayloft. But for me, the Morgans' barn held so many memories, good and bad. I had to keep my eyes on the prize and not get mired in the thoughts of loving and losing Billy. I walked quicker, trying to put the barn and what it symbolized in my rearview.

Halfway to the Morgans' house just past the barn, I ran into Billy. I didn't actually run into him. I stopped dead in my tracks to watch him. He was wearing a skin-tight long-sleeved white thermal shirt and jeans. He'd thrown his jacket onto the pile of logs next to him. The sleeves of his shirt were pushed up and he was swinging an axe, chopping firewood. From behind, I could see the sheer bulk of his lats built up from years of hard work. They rolled and pulled with each swing. His muscular frame was cut from head to toe. I spent my life surrounded by men who had access to the best fitness instructors money could buy and not one of them could hold a candle to Billy. The chiseled shape of a homegrown hunk couldn't be bought—it was hard-earned.

I don't know what possessed me, but I whistled my appreciation.

Billy turned, then smirked.

I couldn't help it. I liked flirting with him. "Do us women-folk a favor and be careful where you're throwing all those muscles around, cowboy."

There was swagger in his reply. "Somebody's gotta manage all this wood. It's not like you've got the chops to pull it off." He winked.

"Very punny. What makes you think I can't handle all of that wood?"

He laughed. I laughed too.

On that note, I turned and headed toward breakfast.

He hollered after me, "Where you goin'?"

I didn't stop or look back, but called to him behind me, "Breakfast."

He had long legs. He'd catch up.

9

BILLY

I t was a rough night. There was not a lot of sleep. After Kat went upstairs, I lingered in the kitchen for a bit. I'd like to say that I was a gentleman and that her melancholy mood dampened my desire for her, but I'd be lying. Even if I was sure that there could be nothing between Kat and I, my dick was not receiving the message. I was the captain in command of a mutinous one-eyed pirate. No matter how many times I pointed out the stormy waters, he continued to search for the booty. I found myself hoping that she wouldn't take a shower. I couldn't bear the thought of knowing that her naked body was behind the bathroom door. Then I realized that no matter what door she was behind, she might be naked, and I considered sleeping on the couch to avoid temptation. I was in a state I hadn't experienced since I was a teenager: Grade A, nonstop boner of steel.

After an hour or so, I felt foolish. I didn't want her to think I was avoiding my own room because she was in the house. Once I was in my room, I didn't know what to do and tried to go to bed. But there was the aforementioned Washington Monument in my boxers. The thing is, I've lived in Kat's house with Wyatt for many years, and I know for a fact the walls are paper-thin. Wyatt does not respect that, so I've heard things I'd like to forget. It was unlikely that Kat would hear me trying to alleviate my situation, but I couldn't risk it.

And then it got worse. Hours went by. I couldn't sleep a wink. I stared at my ceiling, debating whether she fell asleep and if I could finally master debate myself, when I heard her. At first, there was a low moan that cut the silence. And then I heard her begging, "Please..."

When we were young, I used to drive Kat to school. Miriam worked the early shift at the Conway Cafe. Under the guise of having breakfast with Kat, I would leave my house at daybreak and let myself in. Kat did not eat breakfast. She would sleep until the last possible minute. So, I would sneak into her bedroom and have her for breakfast. I teased Kat; I lived to hear her beg for me. And that's what I was hearing. Her voice begging for my tongue. Instantly, my hand was wrapped around my cock, and I followed the rhythm of the sounds she was making until I had a Grade A mess on my hands.

I still couldn't sleep. After a couple of hours of tossing and turning, I figured it was best to just get up. I didn't know what to make of Kat's evening escapes. I didn't know if she was dreaming or if she was just waiting for me to go to sleep like I'd been waiting for her to go to sleep. But I knew for sure I still enjoyed the sound of her. And wanting Kat was too much. I needed to do something physical to regain my composure.

So I went out to the barn, to the woodpile to split logs. I was out there for an hour before Kat whistled at my ass. Any progress I had made in clearing my head of Kat disintegrated. The thing was, I liked Kat flirting with me. And Kat was flirting with me, hard.

When Kat headed into breakfast, so did I. And now, I was sitting at the breakfast table with Wyatt, Kat, and my father. That lazy bastard, Cody, hadn't gotten out of bed yet. Sarah was pouring coffee and slinging bacon and scrambled eggs like it was her job. It took Kat sitting at the table for me to realize that we just assumed that Sarah would cook for us. After Mom passed away, Miriam and Kat had helped out. They shared in the responsibilities of feeding the Morgan boys, but now, it all fell on Sarah's shoulders, and it shouldn't have. I needed to help her. We all needed to help her.

Kat and Sarah were talking about Sarah's gig on Sunday. Sarah said, "If you're still going to be here tomorrow, it would be amazing if you could come to Sadie's."

Kat taught Sarah to play the guitar. I am pretty sure that Sarah looked up to Kat her entire life. It was a pretty big deal when you were a kid from a small town to have grown up with an international superstar. For me, it was a nightmare because everyone felt like I missed out on the gravy train. Sarah, who was a musician, got to say that Kat Bennett helped her write her first song.

"We're not leaving today. I already spoke to my people. So... how about we just say that I'll be there," Kat warmly said.

Sarah's face exploded in a smile. So did mine.

Wyatt interjected. "Are you going to Sarah's show, Bill?"

I never missed Sarah's shows and Wyatt knew it, so he was just meddling. I rolled my eyes at him. "Of course I am, stupid."

"Everyone have biscuits?" Sarah asked.

Kat answered, "No, but Wyatt can get his himself." She was teasing him, but it was like she had read my mind.

Wyatt plastered a smart-ass grin to his face and quipped, "Don't worry, Kat. I know how to butter my own biscuits."

Sarah rolled her eyes. "I am perfectly happy to get your biscuit just so I don't have to hear about your biscuit. Thank you very much."

Kat laughed. Sarah left the room to get the biscuit.

I turned to Wyatt. "We should get our own food."

Wyatt had his mouth full of eggs when he answered, "You should."

"You both should," Kat said.

Wyatt continued to talk with his mouth full. "I do an awful lot around here. We all have a specific set of jobs. I think Sarah's getting off easy scrambling eggs and carrying toast. I do the heavy lifting."

"You do the heavy lifting?" I asked. "I can't remember the last time you lifted anything."

"Heavy lifting is a metaphor, you fool," Wyatt retorted. "I didn't mean that I carry boulders around the farm. I meant that working the ranch is a more grueling job than making lunch."

"Oh, please," Kat snapped. "Sarah absolutely does that too. I could do your job when I was fifteen. I mean, what do you have to do today, Wyatt? Tack a horse and go roam the ranch looking for felled fences? Women are certainly hearty enough to handle that."

"Oh, yeah?" Wyatt questioned. "Do you honestly think you still have what it takes to work a ranch?" At first, it seemed odd that Wyatt was making this argument, but suddenly, I saw where he was heading, and I started to get nervous.

"Absolutely," Kat threw at him without realizing she was falling right into his trap. In our house, a challenge taken had to be proved.

Wyatt smiled, a sneaky little smile. "Well then, I guess you'll have to prove it."

My father laughed out loud. He'd been quiet all through breakfast, as usual. And suddenly, he was sitting at the head of the table rolling out a tremendous belly laugh. "He got you, Kat."

Wyatt brushed the crumbs from his hands onto his lap, stood, and said, "Well, Bill, looks like I got you a new ranch hand today. I'm gonna head back to bed."

10

KAT

illy and I walked side by side toward the barn. The sun had started to break through the clouds, but it was still cold. Anyone who grew up on this ranch knew that the Morgan boys took challenges seriously. It was one of the ways Duke kept his unruly boys in check. If you said you could do it, then you had to prove it or suffer the consequences. So, when Wyatt challenged my sentiments and I confirmed, I was stuck. Otherwise, I had to agree to the idea that a woman was only as valuable as her recipe book. Billy had been quiet ever since Wyatt tricked me into working as a temporary ranch hand. I didn't want to spend the day with him if it was going to make him miserable, but part of me hoped he wanted me close. Either way, it was best to get things out into the open.

"Billy, are you okay with this?" I asked.

He seemed tense but humble when he answered, "I don't want you to feel obligated to help today. I know Wyatt can be..."

"Bullheaded?"

"No..."

"Pompous?"

"No..."

"Endearing?"

He laughed. Then he stopped walking, turned to me, and said, "I realized what he was doing, and I didn't stop him."

It took a second for it to sink in that if Billy didn't stop Wyatt from tricking me into doing his job for the day, then on some level, Billy was saying he wanted to spend the day with me. I stood there flabbergasted. I was shocked by how much I felt. I was shocked that he admitted he wanted to spend the day with me, and I was shocked that spending the day with Billy filled my belly with all kinds of happy butterflies. In response to my dumbfounded expression, Billy offered me an out. "You can just go back to the house. I can handle today on my own."

I turned, headed toward the barn, making sure I was swinging my ass a little, then looked over my shoulder and said, "C'mon, cowboy, we got fences to mend."

He laughed again and moved to catch up with me.

I have to admit, it had been a long time since I had to saddle a horse from start to finish, but it's not something you forget. I wasn't surprised when Billy suggested I ride Teacup, a chestnut brown Appaloosa that the family got when I was sixteen. I'd always enjoyed riding her, but she had a tendency to spin in circles for anyone but me. As Billy led her toward me, he said, "Mostly Sarah rides her now. She doesn't spin for her either."

"Maybe," I offered, "Teacup's cup of tea is ladies?" I put my foot in the stirrup and swung my leg over the saddle. Showing Teacup affection by rubbing her neck, I said, "Is that it, girl? Are you a gal's gal?"

Once he was sure I was settled, Billy handed me Teacup's reins. It should have been nothing, but as he passed the brown leather straps into my hands, our fingertips brushed ever so lightly. That tiny caress rippled through my body like playing a perfect chord on my guitar. Our eyes met. Billy's blues darkened with desire. There was so much history between us. There were so many words we left unsaid. There was so much anger and there was so much love. I couldn't pretend anymore that I only had old feelings for Billy. I always had feelings for him, and I still did. I just pushed them down so deep that I buried a part of myself too.

I reached out and gently ran my fingers across his jawline. His eyes closed at my touch. His stubble was thicker and there were subtle lines at the corners of his eyes. Sweetly, I whispered, "You're older than I remember."

He echoed my tone, "Is that bad?"

"No," I said wistfully. "It's the only thing that feels unfamiliar."

A heavy-hearted look crossed his face. Then he patted my knee, grabbed his hat off the hook on the wall, and moved to mount his own horse, Napoleon.

We spent the day riding side by side. Now that they owned my property, the Morgan ranch sprawled 561 acres. Their original ranch was 500 acres. My grandma sold Duke sixty acres after my grandpa died. My grandpa was never a farmer. He was a mechanic. He bought the land as an investment and let Duke's family use and tend the land for free for years. Then when he died suddenly, Duke overpaid so that my grandma, mom, and I were protected. It only made sense years later that I sold him the house for nothing much. I didn't need the money.

Five hundred sixty-one acres was an average size ranch, but on the back of a horse on a snowy day, it's a lot of rolling white land. Mostly, we were circling the property, checking that the storm didn't take down any posts or break the fence line in any other way. Cows had a tendency to sense downed fences and wander off, which was a way more complicated problem than resetting a fence.

As we rode, we talked. We talked about each of Billy's siblings, who they had dated, what they wanted to do with their lives, who he was worried about, who he wasn't. He was as invested in them as he'd always been. Loved each of them so much, even when they frustrated him. We also talked about Duke's reluctance to retire and Billy's frustration that his father still didn't seem to trust him to take over the ranch operations completely. And then Billy said, "So, what's it like being famous?"

As you would expect, being famous was a mixed bag, but I'd been trained to never answer this particular question honestly. Fans don't want to hear that it's hard to be famous. I shrugged. "It's great."

"Really?" he asked, steering Napoleon to the right with a subtle flick of his wrist.

"What's not to love? I get paid to make my music. That's what I wanted, right?" I smiled and moved to encourage Teacup to follow Billy's horse. Billy was quiet for a minute, clearly mulling over what he wanted to say next. I decided to speak first. "Listen, a lot of it is really wonderful. I love what I do. I love the music and most of the time, fans are great. But sometimes it's scary that everyone knows you and sometimes it's a hassle that you can't just walk into a coffee shop and get a cup of coffee. Touring is exhausting and it can get lonely because, when you're the star, you're not really part of the crew. It's hard to be sure that new people aren't just looking for a free ride, and I grew up surrounded by people I trusted, so that's hard to find..." I realized I was rambling.

"You seemed sad last night," he said. "I thought maybe it wasn't all peaches and cream."

"Is anything?" I asked, cynically.

"And what about..." He couldn't seem to find the words.

"What about what?"

"Do you have someone?" he said, lips tight.

"No, I mean, I have..."

"Don't." He seemed to be begging. "Don't tell me about the men you've had, Kat."

I laughed. "You had to have known I've had boyfriends, Billy. It's in the tabloids, for Pete's sake."

He looked embarrassed. "I might have Googled you once or twice. But that doesn't mean we need to talk about it."

"There was never anyone special, really." I paused. "Not like with you." We rode in silence for a few minutes, and then I asked, "What about you? Is there someone in your life?"

"Sure, there've been a few. But the whole town thinks of me as the guy that was in love with Kat Bennett." I'd never thought about that. It never occurred to me that being connected to me would affect how others saw Billy. "Do you know how many times women in bars have come on to me by asking what your favorite sexual position was?"

I started laughing. "That can't be true."

"Oh, it's true," he retorted.

There was a long pause and then, at the same time, we said something I used to say, "Good cowgirls ride on top."

We both broke into real laughter. And then Billy pointed up ahead to a break in the fence and winking at me, he said, "Come on, cowgirl. We got work to do."

11

BILLY

love this woman. That was what I thought every time I looked at her. I loved her when she showed Teacup a little pat of kindness. I loved her when she touched my face in the barn. I loved how interested she was in my siblings as if they were her own. I loved her when she told me no man she'd been with compared to me. I loved her when she made me remember how she loved to ride me. I loved her standing next to me, cold and wet from resetting a fence and still smiling. I always loved her. I always would.

I'd spent the afternoon looking for reasons to touch her. At first, it was just a hand up or a shoulder to lean on as she climbed over a felled fence. And then I was looking for any excuse to touch her. Ranch work isn't usually sexy. Kat had a way about her that made even breathing sexy. Watching her work, the way she used her body, how strong she was and still so graceful, it was exhilarating. But also, there was something about Kat, like she was made for me. I was more fun with Kat. I was lighter. I was alive.

After a particularly gnarly battle with a fence post, I decided we'd done enough mending for one afternoon and headed back to the barn. Honestly, I could tell Kat was cold. She hadn't complained once, but the idea that she was suffering was too much for me to bear. As it became clear that we were headed back to the barn, she asked, "Are we going back in?"

I shrugged. "Done enough for one day."

With a glint in her eye, she dared, "Last one to the barn is a rotten egg."

Before I could even digest what she said, I was watching her mane of red hair race away from me. She was leaning in close to Teacup's neck, just enough to round her ass, so there was no chance I wasn't staring. I was done controlling how I felt. I wanted Kat, even if she left me again.

I chased after her like a man on a mission. She got to the barn first, but I dismounted Napoleon and was next to her before her feet hit the ground.

As she was sliding off Teacup, I caught her from behind, crushing every curve against me until her feet landed and that pert little ass was pushed hard against my cock. I stayed still for a moment, reveling in the feel of her. Running my hands from her waist to her thighs and up again. Her breathing quickened.

I leaned forward, bringing my lips inches from her ear. "I want to be inside you, Kat." Her head fell back against my chest and she released a gasp of pleasure at my words. Teacup clip-clopped a bit next to us.

"Fuck," she breathed. "We have to tie up the horses."

I didn't move. I wasn't losing this moment. She started to shift away to manage Teacup, but I pulled her back flush against my dick. Low, rough, and humid, I whispered against her ear again. "Here's what I want you to do. While I'm dealing with the horses, you are going to climb up to the loft. You're going to spread out a blanket and lie down. I want you to unbutton your jeans and slide your hand under your panties and touch yourself, Kat."

I cupped her breast in my hand and felt her nipple pebble at my touch. I dropped my hand down, popped the button on her jeans, and slipped my fingers inside, dipping them down until I felt the wetness between her folds.

My voice heavy with need, I stroked her clit and said, "I want you to pretend you're me. I want you to tease yourself. I want you still slick and ready to beg when I get up there. Can you do that for me? Can you tease your sweet little pussy?" She started to buck against the tips of my fingers, already aching for me to make her full.

I pressed my lips against the nape of her neck. And then, for the second time in my life, I said, "I'm gonna kiss you now, Kat."

Disentangling myself from her jeans, I spun her around and pushed her back against the stable door. After ten years, I was desperate for her lips. She was hungry and welcoming. I wasn't gentle. I invaded her mouth, and our tongues intertwined as I pushed closer. My hands encircled her ass, pulling her tight against me. Using my hand, I wrapped her left leg around my waist and rutted my cock right where she needed it, knowing and loving that dry humping didn't have to be enough; we were adults and we had the time to do this slowly.

"I'm gonna fuck you, Kat. Do you understand that?" I panted forcefully.

She nodded, unable to form words, her head thrown back, her eyes closed.

"Good," I quieted, and I put her leg down, then kissed her gently. I turned her body toward the loft ladder. She headed straight for it. I meant to be all alpha and whatnot, but watching her walk away, my dick ached for her. I couldn't help myself. I called after her, "I'll be quick."

She turned around, all sweet smiles and ruddy cheeks. "Oh, thank fuck."

I laughed.

Walking backwards, she said, "I missed you, Billy Morgan, missed you on my skin."

God, I missed her too.

12

***

KAT

*H*oly fuck.

Holy fuck.

He hadn't even touched me yet, and I couldn't catch my breath.

I heard him climbing the ladder up to the loft. I followed his instructions to the letter. We'd often come up here before, years ago. I hadn't forgotten how he made me feel here. His fingers deep inside me. He knew I'd remember. I'd never done something like this before, touched myself, knowing that someone was coming to find me, to watch me.

The men I'd been with since Billy were few. I dated a lot and I'd had sex, but nothing like this man who owned my body. The men I'd been with other than Billy were dates, not lovers. Some I dated for weeks or months, but I didn't let them in and certainly never would have listened if they told me what to do. But being with Billy was different. I was his instrument. He knew exactly how to tune me up and make me sing.

I laid the blanket in the back corner of the loft because that's where we used to fool around. Billy walked up slowly. He was barefoot. He must have left his boots downstairs. Even his feet were sexy.

With his eyes on me, every stroke of my finger intensified. I wanted him already. I wanted him always. He was a fire in my blood. He unbuckled his belt, then unbuttoned his jeans. He took his cock in his hand, lazily stroking, his eyes glued to my movements.

"Take your pants off, Kat," he said, his voice heavy and dark with desire, moving so he was standing above me.

My heart was racing. I shimmied out of my jeans, very aware that I was wearing panties from the drawer in my bedroom.

He smiled. "Have I seen those before?"

I laughed nervously. "Maybe."

"I don't want to see them anymore," he commanded.

I slid the lavender cotton over my ankles and tossed them aside. He stood at the bottom edge of the blanket, framed in my view by my knees, his hand stroking his erection. With every lazy stroke, my insides clenched.

"Open wider. Show me." I dropped my knees a little and felt the cool air on my most sensitive parts.

"So sexy," he purred. "I need to be inside you, Kat. I need to feel you all around me." I wanted that, I did. But I wanted him out of control. I wanted him begging and desperate like I was.

I sat up, took off my top, got on my knees, and crawled toward him. When I was close, inches from his hand on his cock, I said, "I want you in my mouth, first." When we were younger, before we had our first time, I used to lick and suck him for hours. I needed the physical connection and pleasure that we denied ourselves otherwise. The feel of him in my mouth, his head passing over my lips, the taste of him on my tongue, the control of his passion, it became something I craved.

And now I wanted that, I wanted to feel him unravel at my command. He was already so hard that I didn't need to suck the length of him. Instead, I swirled my tongue in circles around the tip. He continued to watch my every move, growling his pleasure in low moans. His hands found their way to my head, and he threaded his fingers through my hair. I sucked him into my mouth.

"Fuck, Kat..." He rocked his hips just a little and I took him deeper. "God, I missed your hot dirty mouth ..." he whined as he pulled out, and then physically lifted me from the floor. Once I was standing, he kissed me, deep and fierce, his tongue penetrating my mouth. I used my hands to work the buttons on his shirt as he quickly shed his pants. And then we were both naked. I shuddered at our first real skin-to-skin contact, chills racing down my spine as he lifted me off the ground, huge man hands on my ass, his cock pressed tight against my clit but not inside me. He carried me about three feet until we were supported by a pile of hay bales, and then he took himself in hand and pressed his cock head to the entrance of my pussy. Holding himself there, he asked, "Are you still on the pill?"

I nodded. Then he looked me in the eye and a sweet softness, a kindness, came over his face. "Are you ready, Kit-Kat? Last chance to turn back."

I didn't want to go back, not now, not ever. I nodded again. Then I leaned in and took his mouth in mine. I knew I would love Billy Morgan until the day I died. And I was one hundred percent certain that I wanted him to take me, hard. A couple of sweet kisses later, I said, "Do it. Fuck me until it hurts."

He pushed inside me, and I cried out. I felt the axis of the earth shift. Everything in my life had been tilted off-kilter for an eternity, and suddenly, as he pressed into my flesh, it was all right again. I could feel all of him, thick and velvety deep inside me. His hands still pressed into the flesh of my backside, he used his strength to buck against me and rock even deeper inside. Then, keeping a deliciously torturous slow pace, he began to fuck me.

I looked down and watched him, glistening with my wetness, pull out a little and drive back in. He brought his forehead to mine, and with each stroke of his cock, he panted, "This. Pussy. Is. Mine. Tell. Me. Kit-Kat. Tell me you're mine."

It was. I was. I always had been. I arched my back, feeling little stalks of hay press into my skin, and drove my hips in rhythm with his, giving him what he wanted, freely. "Yours. Always yours."

My orgasm came on quick and hard. I shattered all around him, contracting inside and out. I'd orgasmed this fiercely before, but only with Billy. The intensity was something I'd forgotten. But as soon as it was happening, the memory of this feeling came rushing back as if my mind destroyed all recollections of what orgasms were supposed to feel like so I could function without him.

I'm pretty sure he meant for us to hump all afternoon, but the waves of my orgasm claimed him too, and I watched the muscles in his face contract as he surrendered. When we stopped, a tangle of satiated limbs, we were suddenly laughing. Not at anything in particular, just roaring with happiness. He kissed me gently and ran his hands over my skin. Everything about him felt calm and peaceful. He picked me up and carried me to the blanket.

"Weren't we supposed to do something on this blanket?" he asked, laying me down and spooning behind me.

"No sense in wasting a good blanket in a hayloft. We'll have to rest up and put it to good use."

"Are you cold?" he asked.

"Hmm..." I was so comfortable in his arms. "No. I'm good."

Deep down in my core, there was a tiny piece of me that wondered if this could all be real. Could it be possible that Billy and I found our way back to each other this easily? Could we just move forward without processing the past? I mean, clearly, we were still physically fated, but could we truly love each other again?

He pulled me closer, nuzzled his nose into the nape of my neck, and his breathing started to slow. In a sleepy haze, he said, "I missed you, too."

13

BILLY

I woke up around dusk from what seemed like the best dream ever. But it wasn't a dream. Kat was still lying next to me, asleep, soft and warm, cuddled against me. Her mane of red hair tickled my chin. She still smelled of lavender, but now, it was supplemented by the salty sweat that lingered in the air. Sex with Kat was unparalleled, even compared to ten years ago. We had changed; we were more confident. I don't know if I would ever see anything as sexy as her lying there waiting for me, naked and wet. And then, with my cock thrust inside her, she said she was mine.

Was she really mine? Or was she just caught up in the heat of the moment? I didn't know what any of this meant. Where did we go from here? We still had the same problems we'd always had. Kat's life was centered around her career and New York, and I was tied to this ranch. But I was different now. Knowing what it was like to live without her, I would compromise in some way. I had to. We had to live apart, but we could see each other. That sounded terrible, but something was better than nothing. I couldn't imagine going back into the darkness of a life without her light.

Behind me, in the pile of Kat's clothes, her phone started to ding. It was a loud bell sound, and I didn't want her to be bothered, so I jumped up to silence it. I rifled through her things and found the phone in her jeans pocket. Before I pressed the buttons to quiet the sound, I noticed the text message that had popped up on the front screen.

June: *Good News. Wheels up tomorrow. Noon.*

My heart started to race and my stomach curdled. Kat was leaving tomorrow. That first day we ran into her, she told Wyatt that she had to get back to New York. If it weren't for the snowstorm, she wouldn't be here at all, and now she was leaving again. She promised Sarah that she'd go to her concert at Sadie's tomorrow night. Guess not.

What was I doing? Kat was an international rock star. There was no life for us together, and no matter how much that killed me, I absolutely could not tolerate her letting down the other people in my family. I couldn't let any of them feel the way I felt for the last ten years. Getting burned by Kat Bennett was not something you get over. She scars you for life.

I looked at her, naked, lying on the blanket in my hayloft, and I just felt so angry. So angry that she left me, so angry she came back, so angry that I couldn't have her, but also so mad that she was about to use the excuse of her music to let Sarah down.

I crossed to my clothes, grabbed my jeans, pulled them on, buttoned them up, and buckled my belt. I felt like her naked body was a weapon she could yield against me, like I couldn't resist her. But maybe with my jeans, I'd be less exposed, like having my dick encased in denim might keep my big head in control when Kat woke up. Stewing, I sat down on a hay bale across from Kat's feet and waited. With each passing minute, my anger grew.

I faltered for a moment when, with her eyes still closed, she pawed behind her, looking for me in her half-awake state, but then I considered the disappointment Sarah was going to feel when she found out that Kat was leaving before her show and my rage solidified. Kat's eyes popped open and she sat up, looking for me. My ire must have been written all over my face because any semblance of the lazy peace she had when waking disappeared.

"Tell me, how was this supposed to work, Kat?" My voice was tight and bitter.

She curled her knees into her chest in an attempt to cover her nakedness and then shifted so she could wrap the blanket around her. She hadn't had time to get angry like me, so the cool and the ugly in my tone hit her like a slap.

"I ... I ..." she stuttered. "I ... don't know exactly. But we can figure it out. Can't we?"

"I'm pretty certain that I remember this part," I spat. "I want you to stay and you have to leave. Isn't that how this works?"

Kat was a firecracker; it didn't take much to ignite her spirit for better or worse. So she quickly found her footing and snapped back, "I do have to leave, Billy. I have commitments elsewhere, but just like ten years ago, that doesn't mean we can't make this work. Or if you want, I can go, and you cannot call me again. As I remember it, that's how this works, isn't it?"

"Fuck you, Kat."

"Too late, you already did."

I turned to leave, but then I stopped. I couldn't help myself. I spun and spat ten years of vitriol at her. "I was nineteen. Nineteen. My mother was dead, and I was responsible for all of my siblings. I couldn't just go racing all over the world with you."

"You never even said that," she yelled. "You just fucking disappeared."

"I needed you and you left."

She was shaking. "I had a contract ... a record deal. I couldn't just walk away from that. But ..."

I interrupted her. "Stop." This was the same old garbage. We would never get out from under this mountain. Her responsibilities to her music would always be more important than me.

I pointed from her to me and me to her. "This is done. It was always done. I'm sorry we entertained the idea of resurrecting it."

"Of course you are," she scoffed.

"What's that supposed to... you know what, forget it. I'm good." I turned again. "Have a nice flight, Kat."

I headed quickly to the ladder.

Behind me, she screamed, "May the wind be at your back, asshole."

It was something she said in a letter that I ignored a long time ago. Barefoot and shirtless, I climbed down from the loft as pissed off as I had ever been. I needed to drive. I grabbed my boots and headed straight for my truck. I couldn't believe I let her do this to me again. I practically flew into the cab of my truck, slammed the door, and peeled out. I didn't know where I was going but as long as it was away from her, it was perfect.

I drove for an hour, determined to get as far away as possible. Never looked back. Never stopped, just drove. Honestly, it was amazing how once you're an experienced driver, you're capable of subconsciously following traffic rules without being truly conscious of what's happening around you. I wasn't thinking of anything specific, just broiling with rage. Eventually, I stopped at a quick mart. I plowed into the store in nothing but my jeans, belt, and boots, and grumbled at the clerk, "You sell clothes?"

He nodded toward a rack of long-sleeved tourist t-shirts, featuring images of Glacier National Park. Fine. Clothes are clothes. I grabbed a bright orange long-sleeved tee with the word Montana scrawled across the front in neon green and pulled it over my head. Then, I booked it to the coolers at the back of the store and grabbed a twelve-pack of beer. I wasn't really a big drinker, but today seemed like as good a day as any to get wasted.

Items paid for, I got back in my truck, turned around, and headed for a rest stop on the freeway about forty minutes outside of Conway. I certainly wasn't going back to chitchat with Kat in her ... correction, in my kitchen. No, thank you. I wanted her good and gone before I went back there again.

And when I got back, I was going to dismantle that fucking bedroom of hers and the rest of it, too. But before I did that, I was going to drink all the beers on my passenger seat and pass out in my truck bed. Now, if I could just erase the look of love on her face when she broke apart all over my cock.

After Billy stormed off, I put on my clothes, climbed out of the hayloft, and looked around, wondering where he went. When he was nowhere to be found, I went back to the house and saw that his truck was gone. I thought to myself, *what am I doing? Why am I doing this to myself?* I knew that when we were making love, he was with me. I felt him connected to my soul, but obviously, it was too much for him. And I wasn't strong enough to go through this with him a second time. So, rather than wait around, I texted June, asked her to send the car, and spent the evening eating takeout and watching *Family Feud* with her and Marcus at the Dew Drop Inn.

Marcus had planned for us to leave Montana at noon. I changed that itinerary as soon as I became aware of it. We were leaving around midnight. There was no way I was missing Sarah's show at Sadie's. I told her I'd be there. Billy knew that, so he could make the decision to be there or not. That wasn't my business. The one thing I had learned in Conway was that I was connected to the Morgans, particularly Sarah, and my screwed-up past with Billy was not going to stop me from caring for them.

I decided to bring Marcus and June with me to Sarah's gig. It was childish. The non-Billy Morgans were like family, but somehow, having my people with me felt right. Also, Marcus was concerned that people in town had gotten wind of the fact that I was around, so a public appearance might require some interference. I couldn't imagine Conwayans all worked up over seeing me. I mean, everywhere else in the world, I was a celebrity, but in Conway, wasn't I just a real person— Kat, the girl who liked to sing, lived with her momma, slung pie at Hazel's, and spent all her free time with Billy Morgan? They all knew who blue-eyed beau was and they never told a single reporter. I couldn't picture them asking for autographs at Sadie's. But I trusted Marcus, and being a celebrity was weird, so it was no harm having him on guard.

We pulled up to Sadie's at six p.m. Sarah went on at six thirty. I scanned the parking lot for Billy's truck. I wanted to be stronger than my feelings for him, but my stomach dropped when I realized he wasn't there. A big piece of my heart thought he'd come riding in, all apologies, and tell me fear had gotten the best of him the day before, but maybe not.

Billy wasn't there, but a tall cowboy with long dirty blond hair and a dark beard was getting out of his truck just a few spaces over. A smile spread across my face. It was Luke. I jumped out of the SUV, with Marcus hollering behind me, and ran toward Luke.

"Patty!" I hollered. It was a nickname from when we were kids. Luke was a vegetarian. Wouldn't eat a steak or a hamburger because he said he couldn't get the heifer's sweet eyes out of his head. So, when you're a vegetarian with parents who own a beef ranch, and your brothers are consummate jerks, your nickname becomes Hamburger Patty, Patty for short. Luke turned in my direction and I jumped into his arms. We hugged tight. Luke was taller and leaner than Billy, but still a bulk of a man.

When we broke apart, he was smiling as wide as me. "What's up, shortstack?" he asked. "I heard you were in town. Thought I might have missed you."

"Never," I said, and he lifted his eyebrows at me, questioning the reality of my comment. I clarified, "Never again."

"Really?" he asked. "Are we finally going to see more of you around here?"

I faltered, not sure how to answer him. Then I decided to tell the truth. "I would love that. I would love to see more of all of you, but Billy and I ..." I let the sentence drop, leaving the ugly to the imagination.

Luke leaned back and rested against the door of his truck. "Bill and you are stupid. It's been ten years—either move on or move in, Kat."

I shook my head at him, then looked at my feet. "It's complicated."

He eyed me for a second, shook his head, and then laughed. "Fools."

I was a touch offended. "There's a lot of water under that bridge. It doesn't just go away."

He put his left arm around me and started us toward the door to Sadie's. "Usually gets worse when you screw without dealing with it, too." My head snapped up and to the right to look at his face. *How did he know that?* He answered my question without me asking it. "You looked at your feet when you were trying to hide your sexcapades when we were kids, too."

"It's nothing," I said, but my voice was tight and sad; even a stranger would have known that sleeping with Billy was a lot more than nothing to me

He huffed out some air and then said, "Kit-Kat, my brother is a shadow of himself since the day you left. It'll never be nothing."

I changed the subject. "Heard you're engaged."

He looked sheepish for a second and then grinned. "She's awesome. Funny, sexy. I mean the whole package. She might come by tonight."

"I'd love to meet her."

"You'll spot her right away. She's got blue hair."

"Wait! I saw her. The day I came to town. She's gorgeous, Luke. Cooler than Conway, though."

He laughed and pulled open the door for me. Sadie's was the same as always. A dark saloon-like space that you might not want to see in the daylight for fear that it was dirtier than you realized. We made our way over to Marcus and June who were standing with Wyatt. Right before we got there, Luke said, "Being honest?"

"Yes, of course." I thought he was going to say something else about Billy.

But instead, he said, "That last album was crap."

It was. I knew it the whole time. I hated the producer. I hated the music. I had nothing I wanted to write about. I forced it and it showed. And somehow, I still felt bad when it got panned. But I shouldn't have. I should know better than to write music on demand. I had to be inspired. I smiled at Luke. "Totally."

"Where's Bill?" Wyatt asked, looking around behind me as if he expected us to show up together.

Luke shrugged. Wyatt looked at me. I could see that he was hopeful that I'd know. "Why would I know?" I asked.

Wyatt's face fell. "Well, shit," he said. "Thought I had that one in the bag."

Cody approached, clearly coming from helping Sarah get set up. He put his hand out to Wyatt. "Twenty bucks, loser."

I looked between the two of them. "Did you two bet on whether Billy and I would come here together?"

Luke sucker punched Wyatt in the arm, and then he looked to Marcus and pointed to Cody. "Could you punch that one for me?"

"What?" Wyatt teased, rubbing his bicep. "It was a good bet. No one got hurt and it could go either way." I rolled my eyes at him. "At least I was on the side of love," he argued, and pointing to Cody, said, "He bet on a future of continued forlornness. He's the real jerk if you ask me."

Wyatt was all jest. And I wasn't angry. I just felt sad. And it must have shown on my face because suddenly, he was crossing the circle of people we were talking to and crushing me to his chest in a big bear hug. "Oh shit, Kat. I'm sorry. He's an idiot."

Cody lifted his glass. "To my eldest brother, the idiot who let the prettiest, most talented, kindest, most spirited woman to ever come out of Conway, Montana, get away—may he always know we like her better than him."

I laughed through my tears.

Luke said, "You were ours too. He took you away from us."

"I'm still pissed," said Wyatt.

"Me too," echoed Cody.

Their love fest for me was interrupted by Sarah stepping up to the microphone. I turned toward her and so did her brothers, Marcus, and June. Sarah looked beautiful, even with no makeup. Her long chestnut hair was free-flowing down her back; she was wearing a cream-colored blouse, jeans, and a pair of purple cowboy boots, which I knew had belonged to her mom. I dreamed about owning those boots when I was a teenager. I was glad Sarah had them.

Sarah started the set with a song. It was obviously an original, and it was good. When I left, she was still a girl and her voice was the voice of a child, but now she had a moody jazz quality that I loved. The song she was singing was about thinking you had strength but feeling untested.

Marcus leaned in behind me. "She's good," he said. I knew that tone. He saw something in Sarah, and I saw it too. When the song was finished, the room exploded in applause.

"Good evening, Conway," Sarah said. "As I'm sure many of you have noticed, we have a special guest in the house tonight."

Someone in the crowd whooped, "Kat Bennett."

I blushed.

As expected, no one had treated me like a star, but clearly, they knew I was here.

Sarah continued. "I am so honored that she's here to see me sing. As many of you know, Kat taught me to play..."

"Oh my God," Cody said behind me. "Like how many times is she gonna tell everyone that?" I couldn't see him, but I could feel him rolling his eyes.

"She also helped me write my first song, which I never sing because it's personal..."

I knew the song. It was a sad, sweet ballad that we wrote together. It was a song about Sarah's loss and her heartbreak when Molly died.

"But I thought tonight, maybe she'd come up here and sing it with me."

I did. And I immediately knew I wanted Sarah's song with her singing lead on my next album. It would be a big choice for her because singing on my record would make her a star.

15

BILLY

For the first time ever, I didn't see Sarah sing. I wanted to blame Kat, but honestly, I was the one who chose not to go, and I felt like a real shit. I just couldn't watch Sarah, heartbroken, up on that dingy little stage at Sadie's, hoping Kat would walk through the door. I also didn't want to be the one to break it to her that Kat wasn't coming.

When I got back to the house on Sunday, Kat was long gone. My mouth was dry, and every little sound was bouncing around in my head like marbles off glass. I'd clearly had way too many pity beers and was monumentally hungover. So, I climbed up the stairs and crashed into my bed. I spent the whole day wallowing, tossing and turning. Sometime in the evening, I showered. I was straight-up broken and not ready to see anyone, so I didn't go to Sadie's. I gave myself one day. One day to drown in utter self-pity, and then it was back to work.

But now it was Monday, and my life was back to what it was before Kat showed up and turned everything on its head. I was Billy Morgan, the somber older brother to four siblings who needed me. The guy who labeled his lunch and kept his socks and underwear in color-coordinated rows because he couldn't have too many idle minutes without feeling crushed by his own losses. I was a cowboy who ran a ranch for my dad and that was my life, plain and simple.

I decided to walk to breakfast. I needed a minute of crisp Montana air before my siblings berated me for missing Sarah's show. I would take the heat. Or maybe I'd get lucky and they'd all be consoling Sarah and dissing Kat because she didn't show. Either way, it was going to be a morning of heated and frank conversation and the air on the way there would give me the opportunity to approach them with a clear head.

I wanted to make sure that everyone understood Kat and I were not an item anymore. We hadn't been in ten years, no matter what any of us had been holding on to. It didn't matter that I knew I would never love a woman the way I loved Kat. I had a place and a family. I made my choice ten years ago.

I was surprised to see Luke's truck parked outside our dad's house. Since he fell for Maddie, he didn't usually come for breakfast. As I pulled open the back door to the kitchen, I heard laughter. The crowd I was walking into was unusually jovial. But when they turned and saw me, all their smiles dropped.

Wyatt spoke first. "Well, if it isn't the stupidest motherfucker I ever saw."

I didn't give him much of a look. Just rolled my eyes and crossed the room, headed for the coffee pot. Sarah blocked me.

"Oh no, big brother. You want coffee, then you best go on back to your house and make yourself some. I'm not doing anything for you for quite some time."

That was a little intense. The coffee was already made, and our other brothers had missed her shows before. "Come on, Sarah. I'm sorry. I should have been there."

"Damn right, you should have," Luke said from behind me. "You broke her fucking heart."

I felt terrible. I really didn't realize that Sarah was going to be so upset if I missed her show. And my brothers all seemed so worked up. Actually, they were all being a little ridiculous. For fuck's sake, I did everything for them. Everything. I was giving up the woman I loved for this motley crew, and I missed one show of Sarah's and they were all jumping down my throat. I tried to keep my rage in check, but it was boiling over.

"Give me a fucking break, okay? I needed time to myself. Am I ever allowed a little time to myself?"

My father walked into the room. He didn't look at me. Sarah poured him a cup of coffee and handed it to him. He took the cup and walked out without acknowledging me at all.

I pointed after him. "What the hell was that? Is he pissed at me too?"

Wyatt of all people was calm. "We're not pissed. We're just disappointed."

Cody, who was filling his plate with eggs, asked, "I just don't get it, Bill. Who wouldn't want that woman? She's smokin', she's successful, she's fun. What's not to like?"

Wait a minute. What? I stood there a little dumbfounded. I tried to figure out what the hell was happening with my siblings. Were they mad at me because Kat didn't show? Did they think I ran her off? That was totally unfair. I tried to clarify. "Are y'all on my back right now because I didn't come to Sarah's show last night? Or because Kat didn't come to Sarah's show? Because that wasn't my fault. She was always leaving. I had nothing to do with it."

Sarah's lip trembled and she looked at me with such pity.

"Oh, Jesus," Wyatt said.

"Fool," Luke said.

Cody started laughing.

"What?" I asked.

Sarah was the one who spoke up. "She was there, Bill. She didn't miss a minute."

I felt like the floor fell out from under me. "She couldn't have been," I said pathetically. "I saw the text on her phone."

"She sang with me, Bill," Sarah said.

"The text said, *'wheels up, noon.'* I saw it," I insisted, horrified at my hasty assumptions.

Wyatt rolled his eyes. "She's a megastar with her own plane, dude."

I dropped my face into my hands. I had her. She was mine again and I pushed her away. I couldn't help myself. "*Fuck!*" I screamed.

"*Language!*" my father hollered from the dining room.

All of my siblings laughed. My father was always trying to curb our language, but I'd been ranching with him my whole life and if he adhered to his own rules, then his mouth would have constantly tasted like soap.

Luke hollered back at him, "He thought she left before the show, Dad."

I heard him push his chair out and he came into the kitchen. "Well, fuck."

I felt absolutely desperate. "What the hell am I gonna do?"

My father smiled. "You're gonna go get your girl."

16

KAT

On the plane from Conway to New York, I wrote three songs. Three. That was one more song than I'd written in the previous year. One weekend at home and I had three songs worth of things to say. Sure, they were full of angst and sadness, but I could hear the music again. I got off the plane and went straight to the studio. It was the same the last time Billy broke my heart. I threw myself into the music and eventually, instead of drowning, I felt like there was enough oxygen to tread water. I never really recovered, but maybe that wasn't my story. Maybe I did choose my career. Maybe you didn't get to have it all.

Billy tried to call. I ignored his calls. He left messages. I couldn't give him a chance to do more damage. Obviously, he had ten years of pent-up anger that he couldn't move past. I could break down in tears every time I thought about how we'd broken each other.

When the phone rang for the fifth time, I handed it to June. "Put it in your purse. Silence it. Anyone who really needs me will call you or Marcus."

She nodded and took the phone. There is a certain freedom to being disconnected. Sometimes that constant connection to the outside world can be really counterproductive for an artist. In turn, being phone-free can be invigorating. I asked Marcus to bring in my favorite producer, Josh Devrow, and I spent three days locked in, making really good music. I didn't come up for air until Thursday morning.

My entire team clapped as I left the studio.

"You found it," Marcus said. "The voice I heard on the stage in Bozeman all those years ago, she's back."

I felt that. I knew the music was right again, and the energy of that was supposed to be magical, but I'd give it all back. If I could rewind, I would never have gotten on the plane ten years ago. The music mattered. It did. But I made music in Conway. People loved to hear me perform there. Did I really need all this? The fame? The celebrity status? The fans? The entourage? Wasn't I happier being just a normal girl with my guitar and my blue-eyed beau?

June put her arm around me as we walked toward the elevator. "You okay, Kat?"

I didn't lie. "Not really."

"The music is good when the heart is a mess." She sighed.

"Pretty much."

"You could talk to him," she suggested.

A tear slipped out. I'd been doing my best not to cry about Billy, but I was worn out. I wiped it quickly. "I don't want to. Ten years ago, when I came to New York, I called. And he didn't care. Now, I let him in again and got burned. Fool me once and all that."

"So, you just want it to be over?" she asked. Her voice seemed tense like she was worried.

We stepped into the elevator as I said, "I mean, I don't know. I'm just exhausted. I want him to fight for me, ya know? Like all these years, my sin was leaving, right? I left him, but honestly, what eighteen-year-old musician wouldn't grab her lottery ticket? That's what Marcus offered me all those years ago, a winning lottery ticket."

Pressing the button for the lobby, June agreed. "No one would have turned that down. You were a star in the making."

"I thought I could have everything. I mean, I thought he'd come around. I thought I'd come home one day and he'd just be standing at my door with roses." I laughed. "I mean, I pictured him, a brawny man in his ten-gallon hat, fighting with my doorman. For years. Literally for years, I kept thinking he'd just white knight it and show up. But it's ten years later, and he still can't imagine a way to make it work. I have all the money in the world... We could have found a solution, but he couldn't handle it."

"Well, what if he could?" June asked.

"Maybe..."

The elevator doors opened. And there he was. Roses. Ten-gallon hat. The whole shebang. Billy Morgan, consummate rancher, standing in the lobby of LSA Records in Manhattan, New York.

I didn't believe it at first. He looked tired and rumpled, like he'd been through the ringer. There were dark circles under his eyes, and I just knew. He was as miserable as I was. His apology was written all over his face. My heart leaped in my chest, racing like it knew it belonged closer to him, but my brain kept me in place.

"Billy?" I asked, my voice shaking and shattered.

"I love you," he said. "I've been sitting here in this lobby and waiting outside your apartment trying to find the words to explain my stupidity for the last two days, and I will explain. I need to. But the thing is, none of it matters. There are no excuses. I'm just so sorry, Kit-Kat. And the long and short of it is, I love you. I love you so fucking much that when you're not near me, I'm dying."

I still couldn't quite believe this was happening. "What about your family and the ranch?"

He took another step closer. "They'll figure it out, Kat. They want me with you."

My lips started to tremble, and I couldn't stop the tears running down my face. "You want to be here with me?"

"Always with you."

I stood there, crying sappy, happy tears.

He took a final step so that we were standing toe to toe and said, "I'm gonna kiss you now, Kat."

And he did.

Finally, my blue-eyed beau was mine again.

WANT to read more about the Morgans, and learn what happens to Kat and Billy in the future? Check out *Imperfect Harmony*, the next book in The Big Sky Cowboys series.

ALSO BY LOLA WEST

Check Out the Big Sky Cowboy Series

Tofu Cowboy

Her Comeback (Oct 2020)

Imperfect Harmony (Nov 2020)

Wild Child (Dec 2020)

Her First Rodeo (Jan 2021)

Hot for the Holidays

Mistletoe in Malibu (Nov 2020)

ABOUT THE AUTHOR

Lola West writes short, sweet, smart, silly, sexy romance. With a PhD in woman's studies and a flair for the dramatic, Lola likes to keep it real. Her loves are cotton candy, astronomy, kitten heels and small-town hunks. Lola's heroes make you swoon and her heroines talk back. Also, she believes that consent is always sexy, even in books.

You can learn more about Lola by visiting lolawestromance.com and find a **FREE BOOK,** a prequel to the Big Sky Cowboys Series or find her hanging out all over the internet.

Find that you're suddenly a Lola West Fan
Follow Lola on Instagram
Follow Lola on Facebook
Follow Lola on Goodreads
Follow Lola on Bookbub
Hang with Lola in the private Facebook group:
Sugary Sweet & Lots of Heat

DID YOU LOVE HER COMEBACK?

Dear Reader,

I would be ever so grateful if you would take five minutes and write me a review. I want to hear your opinions. Also, good reviews on Bookbub, Goodreads, or Amazon let other people know that mine is a book worth reading. Reviews mean book sales, and sales mean I can continue to write books for you!

Thank you in advance.

XO,

Lola

Made in the USA
Columbia, SC
08 July 2023

19946390R00107